'Earth's got the power to wipe clean every other humanly-settled world whenever she wants to. When Earth moves, when she decides to move, you'll vanish.' He paused. She still sat, not speaking.

'There's no reprieve, no choice. The politicians haven't announced it yet – but the Dorsai is already a forgotten world.'

'General,' said Amanda. 'I've listened to you. Now you listen to me. You're the one who's dreaming. You're already defeated. You just don't know it.'

'Mrs Morgan, you're a fool. There's no way you can defeat Earth.'

'Yes,' said Amanda, bleakly. 'Believe me, there is.'

The Spirit of Dorsai

GORDON R. DICKSON

SPHERE BOOKS LIMITED

SPHERE BOOKS LTD

Published by the Penguin Group
27 Wrights Lane, London W8 5TZ, England
Viking Penguin Inc., 40 West 23rd Street, New York, New York 10010, USA
Penguin Books Australia Ltd, Ringwood, Victoria, Australia
Penguin Books Canada Ltd, 2801 John Street, Markham, Ontario, Canada L3R 1B4
Penguin Books (NZ) Ltd, 182–190 Wairau Road, Auckland 10, New Zealand

Penguin Books Ltd, Registered Offices: Harmondsworth, Middlesex, England

First published in Great Britain by Sphere Books Ltd 1983
Reprinted 1985, 1987, 1989

A portion of this book was published as
'Brothers' in *Astounding: John W. Campbell
Memorial Anthology*, copyright © 1973 by
Random House, Inc.

Printed and bound in Great Britain by
Richard Clay Ltd, Bungay, Suffolk

This book is dedicated to my grandmother,
Mary Elizabeth Ford and to my great-
grandmother, Margaret Minteer

CONTENTS

Prologue

She was tall, slim, and so blonde as to be almost white-haired. There was an erectness to her body that no man could have possessed without stiffness. As she sat cross-legged, her grey eyes gazing down into the valley on the Dorsai that held Fal Morgan and the surrounding home-steads, her face had the quality of a profile stamped on a silver coin.

'Amanda . . .' said Hal Mayne, gently.

Lost in her thoughts, she did not hear him; and the moment was so close to perfection that he was reluctant to disturb it. The part of him that was a poet, which had survived the months of being a hunted guerrilla on Harmony and even the sickness and the brutalities of the prison there before his escape, stirred again, watching her. Here, on the roof of a warrior's world, under a clean and cloudless sky in a time when the human race was everywhere submitting to the chains of a new slavery, she wore an armor of sunlight, unconquerable. Beside her, in his much taller, wide-shouldered but gaunt, body, pared thin by privation and suffering, he felt like some great dark bird of earth-bound flesh and bone, bending above an entity of pure spirit.

As he waited, her eyes lost their abstraction. As if they had been separated so far that his voice, speaking her name, had had to stretch across time and space to only now reach her, she turned finally back to him.

'Did you say something?' she asked.

'I was going to say how much you resemble that picture of her – of the first Amanda Morgan,' he said. 'It could be a picture of you.'

3

She smiled a little.

'Yes,' she said, 'both the second Amanda to bear the name, and I look very much like her. It happens.'

'It's still a strange thing, with only three of you of that name in your family in two hundred years,' he said. 'Does it just happen she had her picture printed at the same age you are now?' he said.

'No.' She shook her head. 'It wasn't.'

'It wasn't?'

'No. That picture you saw in our hall was made when she was much older than I am now.'

He frowned.

'It's true,' she said. 'We age very slowly, we Morgans – and she was something special.'

'Not as special as you,' he said. 'She couldn't be. You're Dorsai – end-result Dorsai. She lived before people like you were what you are now.'

'That's not true,' the third Amanda said. 'She was Dorsai before there was a Dorsai world. What she was, was the material out of which our people and our culture here were made.'

He shook his head, slowly.

'How can you be so sure about what she was – two hundred standard years ago?'

'How can I?' She looked at him for a moment. 'In many ways, I am her.'

He watched her.

'A reincarnation?'

'No,' she answered. 'Not really. But something . . . more as if time didn't matter. As if it's all the same thing; her, there in the beginning of our world, and I here, at . . .'

'The end of it,' he suggested.

'No.' She looked at him steadily with those grey eyes. 'The end won't be until the last Dorsai is dead. In fact, not even then. The end will only be when the last human is dead – because what makes us Dorsai is something that's a part of all humans; that part the first Amanda

4

had when she was born, back on Earth.'

Something – the shadow of a swooping bird, perhaps – shuttered the sunlight from his eyes for a split second.

'You think so much of her,' he said, thoughtfully. 'But it's Cletus Grahame and his textbooks on the military art he wrote two hundred years ago – it's Donal Graeme and the way he brought the inhabited worlds together, one hundred years ago – that other worlds think of when they use the word "Dorsai".'

'We've had Graemes for our next neighbor since Cletus,' she replied. 'What's thought of them, they earned. But the first Amanda was here before either of them. She founded our family. She cleared the outlaws from these mountains before Cletus came; and when she was ninety-three, she held Foralie district against Dow deCastries' veteran troops when they invaded, thinking they'd have no trouble with the children, the women, the sick and the old that were all that was left here, then.'

'You mean,' Hal said, 'that time deCastries tried to take over the Dorsai, at the very end of Cletus' struggle with him?'

'With him and all the power of Earth behind him, in a time when everyone thought Earth was more powerful than all the other inhabited worlds combined.'

'But wasn't it Cletus who gave directions for the defense of Dorsai, that time?'

'Cletus wasn't here. He left two of his officers, Arvid Johnson and Bill Athyer, to coordinate the defense and give the districts a general survey of the strategical and tactical situations involved. But their job was only a matter of laying out the military physics of the situation, with Cletus' theories and principles as guidelines. It was up to each district individually after that, to draw up its own plan for dealing with the invaders. That's what Foralie did – knowing it would be under the gun more than any other district, since Foralie homestead was here, and Cletus would be expected to return to it as soon as he heard the Dorsai had been invaded.'

5

'And it was the first Amanda who was given charge of Foralie district, by the people in the district, then?' he asked. 'Why her? she hadn't been a soldier.'

'I told you,' she said. 'During the Outlaw Years, she'd led the way in clearing out the lawless mercenaries. After she did that – and other things – with just the women, the cripples, old men and children to help her, the rest of the districts followed her example and law came to all the Dorsai. She was the best person to command.'

'How did they do it, then?'

'Clean out the outlaws?' the third Amanda asked.

'No – though I want to hear that sometime, too. What I meant was, how did Amanda and Foralie district defeat first-line troops? Most military scholars seem to think that the invaders defeated themselves, that they had to defeat themselves; because there was no way a gaggle of women, children and old people could possibly have done it.'

'In a way you could say the troops did defeat themselves – did you ever read Cletus' Tactics of Mistake?' she answered. 'But actually what happened was a case of putting our strengths against the weaknesses of the invaders.'

'Weaknesses? What weaknesses did first-line troops have?'

She looked at him again with those level eyes.

'They weren't willing to die unless they had to.'

'That?' Hal looked at her curiously. 'That's a weakness?'

'Comparatively. Because we were.'

'Willing to die?' he studied her. 'Non-combatants? Old people, mothers–'

'And children. Yes.' The armor of sunlight around her seemed to invest her words with a quality of truth greater than he had ever known from anyone else. 'The Dorsai was formed by people who were willing to pay with their lives in others' battles, in order to buy freedom for their homes. Not only the men who went off to fight, but those

6

at home that had same image of freedom and were willing to live and die for it.'

'But simply being willing to die–'

'You don't understand, not being born here,' she said.
'It was a matter of their being able to make harder choices
than people less willing. Amanda and the others in the
district best qualified to decide sat down and considered a
number of plans. They all entailed casualties – and the
casualties could include the people who were considering
the plans. They chose the one that gave the district the
greatest effectiveness against the enemy for the least
number of deaths; and, having chosen it, they were all
ready to be among those who died, if necessary. The
invading soldiers had no such plan – and no such
courage.'

He shook his head.

'I don't understand,' he said.

'That's because you're not Dorsai. And because you
don't understand someone like the first Amanda.'

'No,' he said. 'That's true. I don't.'

He looked at her.

'How did it happen?' he asked. 'How did she – how did
they do it? I have to know.'

'You do?' Her gaze was unmoving on him.

'Yes,' he said. There were so many things he had not
been able to explain, things he had not admitted to her
yet. There was the matter of his visit to Foralie, and
the particular moment in which he had stepped into the
doorway which some of the towering Graeme men, such
as Ian and Kensie, the twin uncles of Donal Graeme, had
been said to fill from sill to lintel and from side to side. As
it had been with them, Hal's unshod feet had rested on
the sill and the top of his head brushed the lintel. But
unlike them, his shoulder-points had not touched the
frame on either side.

It might be that with recovered health and some years
of growth yet, that, too, could happen. But it did not
matter. What mattered – and what he could not yet

7

bring himself to talk about – was the sudden, poignant, feeling in him of kinship with the Graemes, unexpected as a blow, that had come on him without warning, as he stood in the doorway.

'I need to know,' he said again.

'All right,' she said. 'I'll tell you just how it was.'

Amanda Morgan

Stone are my walls, and my roof is of timber;
But the hands of my builder are stronger by far.
The roof may be burned and my stones may be
scattered.
Never her light be defeated in war . . .
                    Song of the house named Fal Morgan

Amanda Morgan woke suddenly in darkness, her finger
automatically on the firing button of the heavy energy
handgun. She had heard – or dreamed she heard – the cry
of a child. Rousing further, she remembered Betta in the
next room and faced the impossibility of her great-
granddaughter giving birth without calling her. It had
been part of her dream, then.

Still, for a few seconds more, she lay, feeling the ghosts
of old enemies still around her and the sleeping house. The
cry had merged with the dream she had been having. In
her dream, she had been reliving the long-ago swoop on
her skimmer, handgun in fist, down into the first of the
outlaw camps. It had been when Dorsai was new; and
the camps, back in the mountains, had been bases for
the out-of-work mercenaries. She had finally led the
women of Foralie district against these men who had
raided their homes for so long, in the intervals when
the professional soldiers of their own households were
away fighting on other worlds.

The last thing the outlaws had expected from a bunch of
women had been a frontal assault in full daylight. There-
fore, it had been that she had given them. In her dream she
had been recalling the fierce bolts from the handgun slicing

11

through makeshift walls and the bodies beyond, setting fire to dried wood and oily rags.

By the time she had been in among the huts, some of the outlaws were already armed and out of their structures; and the rest of the fight had disintegrated into a mixed blur of bodies and weapons. The outlaws were all veterans – but so, in their own way, were the women from the households. There were good shots on both sides; and in her younger strength, then, she was a match for any out-of-condition mercenary. Also, she was carried along in a rage they could not match . . .

She blinked, pushing the images of the dream from her. The outlaws were gone now – as were the Eversills who had tried to steal her land, and other enemies. They were all gone, now, making way for new foes. She listened a moment longer, but about her the house of Fal Morgan was still.

After a moment she got up anyway, stepping for a second into the chill bath of night air as she reached for a robe from the chair by her bed. Strong moonlight, filtering through sheer curtains, gave back her ghost in dim image from the tall armoire mirror. A ghost from sixty years past. For a second before the robe settled about her, the lean and still-erect shape in the mirror invented the illusion of a young, full-fleshed body. She went out.

Twenty steps down the long panelled corridor, with the familiar silent cone rifles and other combat arms standing like sentries in their racks on either wall, she became conscious of the fact that habit still had the energy handgun in her grasp. She shelved it in the rack and went on to her great-granddaughter's door. She opened it and stepped in.

The moonlight shone through the curtains even more brightly on this side of the house. Betta still slept, breathing heavily, her swollen middle rising like a promise under the covering blankets. The concern about this child-to-be, which had occupied Amanda all these past months, came back on her with fresh urgency. She touched the rough, heavy cloth over the unborn life briefly and lightly with her fingertips. Then she turned and went back out. Down the corridor and around the corner, the Earth-built clock in the living room chimed the first quarter of an hour past four a.m.

She was fully awake now, and her mind moved purposefully. The birth was due at any time now; and Betta was insistent about wanting to use the name Amanda if it was a girl. Was she wrong in withholding it, again? Her decision could not be put off much longer. In the kitchen she made herself tea. Sitting at the table by the window, she drank it, gazing down over the green tops of the conifers, the pines and spruce on the slope that fell away from the side of the house, then rose again to the close horizon of the ridge in that direction, and the mountain peaks beyond, overlooking Foralie Town and Fal Morgan alike, together with a dozen similar homesteads.

She could not put off any longer the making up of her mind. As soon as the baby was born, Betta would want to name her. On the surface, it did not seem such an important matter. Why should one name be particularly sacred? Except that Betta did not realize, none of them in the family seemed to realize, how much the name Amanda had come to be a talisman for them all.

The trouble was, time had caught up with her. There was no guarantee that she could wait around for more children to be born. With the trouble that was probably coming, the odds were against her being lucky enough to still be here for the official naming of Betta's child, when that took place. But there had been a strong reason behind her refusal to let her name be given to one of the younger generations, all these years. True, it was not an easy reason to explain or defend. Its roots were in something as deep as a superstition – the feeling in her that Fal Morgan would only stand as long as that name in the family could stand like a pillar to which they could all anchor. And how could she tell ahead of time how a baby would turn out?

Once more she had worn a new groove around the full circle of the problem. For a few moments, while she drank

13

her tea, she let her thoughts slide off to the conifers below, which she had stretched herself to buy as seedlings when the Earth stock had finally been imported here to this world they called the Dorsai. They had grown until now they blocked the field of fire from the house in that direction. During the Outlaw Years, she would never have let them grow so high.

With what might be now coming in the way of trouble from Earth, they should probably be cut down completely – though the thought of it went against something deep in her. This house, this land, all of it, was what she had built for herself, her children and their children. It was the greatest of her dreams, made real; and there was no part of it, once won, that she could give up easily.

Still seated by the window, slowly drinking the hot tea, her mind went off entirely from the threats of the present to her earliest dreams, back to Caernarvon and the Wales of her childhood, to her small room on a top floor with the ceiling all angles.

She remembered that, now, as she sat in this house with only two lives presently stirring between its walls. No – three, with the child waiting to be born, who would be having dreams of her own, before long. How old had she herself been when she had first dreamed of running the wind?

That had been a very early dream of hers, a waking dream – also invoked as she was falling asleep. So that with luck, sometimes, it became a real dream. She had imagined herself being able to run at great speed along the breast of the rolling wind, above city and countryside. In her imagination she had run barefoot, and she had been able to feel the texture of the flowing air under her feet, that was like a soft, moving mattress. She had been very young. But it had been a powerful thing, that running.

In her imagination she had run from Caernarvon and Cardiff clear to France and back again; not above great banks of solar collectors or clumps of manufactories, but over open fields and mountains and cattle, and over flowers in fields where green things grew and where people were happy. She had gotten finally so that she could run, in her imagination, farther and faster than anyone.

None was so fleet as she. She ran to Spain and Norway. She ran across Europe as far as Russia, she ran south to the end of Africa and beyond that to the Antarctic and saw the great whales still alive. She ran west over America and south over South America. She saw the cowboys and gauchos as they once had been, and she saw the strange people at the tip of South America where it was quite cold.

She ran west over the Pacific, over all the south Pacific and over the north Pacific. She ran over the volcanos of the Hawaiian islands, over Japan and China and Indo-China. She ran south over Australia and saw deserts, and the great herds of sheep and the wild kangaroos hopping.

Then she went west once more and saw the steppes and the Ukraine and the Black Sea and Constantinople that was, and Turkey, and all the plains where Alexander marched his army to the east, and then back to Africa. She saw strange ships with lug sails on the sea east of Africa, and she ran across the Mediterranean where she saw Italy. She looked down on Rome, with all its history, and on the Swiss alps where people yodeled and climbed mountains when they were not working very hard; and all in all she saw many things, until she finally ran home and fell asleep on the breast of the wind and on her own bed. Remembering it all, now that she was ninety-two years old – which was a figure that meant nothing to her – she sat here, light years from it all, on the Dorsai, thinking of it all and drinking tea in the last of the moonlight, looking down at her conifers.

She stirred, pushed the empty cup from her and rose. Time to begin the day – her control bracelet chimed with the note of an incoming call.

She thumbed the bracelet's com button. The cover over the phone screen on the kitchen wall slid back and the screen itself lit up with the heavy face of Piers van der Lin. That face looked out and down at her, the lines that time had cut into it deeper than she had ever seen them. A sound of wheezing whistled and sang behind the labour of his speaking.

'Sorry, Amanda,' his voice was hoarse and slow with both age and illness. 'Woke you, didn't I?'

'Woke me?' She felt a tension in him and was suddenly alert. 'Piers, it's almost daybreak. You know me better than that. What is it?'

'Bad news, I'm afraid . . .' his breathing, like the faint distant music of war-pipes, sounded between words. 'The invasion from Earth is on its way. Word just came. Coalition first-line troops – to reach the planet here in thirty-two hours.'

'Well, Cletus told us it would happen. Do you want me down in town?'

'No,' he said.

Her voice took on an edge in spite of her best intentions.

'Don't be foolish, Piers,' she said. 'If they can take away the freedom we have here, then the Dorsai ceases to exist – except for a name. We're all expendable.'

'Yes,' he said, wheezing, 'but you're far down on the list. Don't be foolish, yourself, Amanda. You know what you're worth to us.'

'Piers, what do you want me to do?'

He looked at her with a face carved by the same years that had touched her so lightly.

'Cletus just sent word to Eachan Khan to hold himself out from any resistance action here. That leaves us back where we were to begin with in a choice for a Commander for the district. I know, Betta's about due –'

'That's not it.' She broke in. 'You know what it is. You ought to. I'm not that young any more. Does the district want someone who might fold up on them?'

'They want you, at any cost. You know that,' Piers said, heavily. 'Even Eachan only accepted because you asked someone else to take it. There's no one in the district, no matter what their age or name, who won't jump when you speak. No one else can say that. What do you think they

16

care about the fact you aren't what you were, physically? They want you.'

Amanda took a deep breath. She had had a feeling in her bones about this. He was going on.

'I've already passed the word to Arvid Johnson and Bill Athyer – those two Cletus left behind to organize the planet's defense. With Betta as she is, we wouldn't have called on you if there was any other choice – but there isn't, now –'

'All right,' said Amanda. There was no point in trying to dodge what had to be. Fal Morgan would have to be left empty and unprotected against the invaders. That was simply the way of it. No point, either, in railing against Piers. His exhaustion under the extended asthmatic attack was plain. 'I'll be glad to if I'm really needed, you know that. You've already told Johnson and Athyer I'll do it?'

'I just said I'd ask you.'

'No need for that. You should know you can count on me. Shall I call and tell them it's settled?'

'I think . . . they'll be contacting you.'

Amanda glanced at her bracelet. Sure enough, the tiny red phone light on it was blinking – signalling another call in waiting. It could have begun that blinking any time in the last minute or so; but she should have noticed it before this.

'I think they're on the line now,' she said. 'I'll sign off. And I'll take care of things, Piers. Try and get some sleep.'

'I'll sleep . . . soon,' he said. 'Thanks, Amanda.'

'Nonsense.' She broke the connection and touched the bracelet for the second call. The contrast was characteristic of this Dorsai world of theirs – sophisticated com equipment built into a house constructed by hand, of native timber and stone. The screen grayed and then came back into color to show an office room all but hidden by the largeboned face of a blond-haired man in his middle twenties. The single barred star of a vice-marshall glinted on the collar of his grey field uniform. Above it was a face that might have been boyish once, but now had a stillness

17

to it, a quiet and waiting that made it old before its time.

'Amanda ap Morgan?'

'Yes,' said Amanda. 'You're Arvid Johnson?'

'That's right,' he answered. 'Piers suggested we ask you to take on the duty of Commander of Foralie District.'

'Yes, he just called.'

'We understand,' Arvid's eyes in the screen were steady on her, 'your great-granddaughter's pregnant –'

'I've already told Piers I'd do it.' Amanda examined Arvid minutely. He was one of the two people on which they must all depend – with Cletus Grahame gone. 'If you know this district, you know there's no one else for the job. Eachan Khan could do it, but apparently that son-in-law of his just told him to keep himself available for other things.'

'We know about Cletus asking him to stay out of things,' said Arvid. 'I'm sorry it has to be you –'

'Don't be sorry,' said Amanda. 'I'm not doing it for you. We're all doing it for ourselves.'

'Well, thanks anyway.' He smiled, a little wearily.

'As I say, it's not a matter for thanks.'

'Whatever you like.'

Amanda continued to examine him closely, across the gulf of the years separating them. What she was seeing, she decided, was that new certainty that was beginning to be noticable in the Dorsai around Cletus. There was something about Arvid that was as immovable as a mountain.

'What do you want me to do first?' she asked.

'There's to be a meeting of all district commanders of this island at South Point, at 0900 this morning. We'd like you here. Also, since Foralie's the place Cletus is going to come back to – if he comes back – you can expect some special attention; and Bill and I would like to talk to you about that. We can arrange pickup for you from the Foralie Town airpad, if you'll be waiting there in an hour.'

Amanda thought swiftly.

'Make it two hours. I've got things to do first.'

'All right. Two hours, then, Foralie Town airpad.'

18

'Don't concern yourself,' said Amanda. 'I'll remember.'

She broke the connection. For a brief moment more she sat, turning things over in her mind. Then she rang Foralie homestead, home of Cletus and Melissa Grahame.

There was a short delay, then the narrow-boned face of Melissa – Eachan Khan's daughter, now Cletus' wife – took shape under touseled hair on the screen. Melissa's eyelids were still heavy with sleep.

'Who – oh, Amanda,' she said.

'I've just been asked to take over district command, from Piers,' Amanda said. 'The invasion's on its way and I've got to leave Fal Morgan in an hour for a meeting at South Point. I don't know when or if I'll be back. Can you take Betta?'

'Of course.' Melissa's voice and face were coming awake as she spoke. 'How close is she?'

'Any time.'

'She can ride?'

'Not horseback. Just about anything else.'

Melissa nodded.

'I'll be over in the skimmer in forty minutes.' She looked out of the screen at Amanda. 'I know – you'd rather I moved in with her there. But I can't leave Foralie, now. I promised Cletus.'

'I understand,' said Amanda. 'Do you know yet when Cletus will be back?'

'No. Any time – like Betta.' Her voice thinned a little. 'I'm never sure.'

'No. Nor he, either, I suppose.' Amanda watched the younger woman for a second. 'I'll have Betta ready when you get here. Goodby.'

'Goodby.'

Amanda broke contact and set about getting Betta up and packed. This done, there was the house to be organized for a period of perhaps some days without inhabitants. Betta sat bundled in a chair in the kitchen, waiting, as Amanda finished programming the automatic controls of the house for the interval.

'You can call me from time to time at Foralie,' Betta said.

'When possible,' said Amanda.

She glanced over and saw the normally open, friendly face of her great-granddaughter, now looking puffy and pale above the red cardigan sweater enveloping her. Betta was more than capable in ordinary times; it was only in emergencies like this that she had a tendency to founder. Amanda checked her own critical frame of mind. It was not easy for Betta, about to have a child with her husband, father and brother all off-planet, in combat, and – the nature of war being what it was – the possibility existing that none of them might come back to her. There were only three men at the moment, left in the house of ap Morgan, and only two women; and now one of those two, Amanda, herself, was going off on a duty that could end in a hangman's rope or a firing squad. For she did not delude herself that the Earth-bred Alliance and Coalition military would fight with the same restraint toward civilians the soldiers of the younger worlds showed.

But it would not help to fuss over Betta now. It would help none of them – there was an approaching humming noise outside the house that crescendoed to a peak just beyond the kitchen door, and stopped.

'Melissa,' said Betta.

'Come on,' Amanda said.

She led the way outside. Betta followed, a little clumsily, and Melissa with Amanda helped her into the open cockpit of the ducted fan skimmer.

'I'll check up on you when I have time,' Amanda said, kissing her great-granddaughter briefly. Betta's arms tightened fiercely around her.

'*Mandy!*' The diminutive of her name which only the young children normally used and the sudden desperate appeal in Betta's voice sent a surge of empathy arcing between them. Over Betta's shoulder, Amanda saw the face of Melissa, calm and waiting. Unlike Betta, Melissa came into her own in a crisis – it was in ordinary times that the daughter of Eachan Khan fumbled and lost her way.

'Never mind me,' said Amanda, 'I'll be all right. Take care of your own duties.'

With strength, she freed herself and waved them off. For a second more she stood, watching their skimmer hum off down the slope. Betta's farewell had just woken a grimness in her that was still there. Melissa and Betta. Either way, being a woman who was useful half the time was no good. Life required you to be operative at all hours and seasons.

That was the problem with a talisman-name like her own. She who would own it must be operative in just that way, at all times. When someone of that capability should be born into the family, she could release the name of Amanda, which she had so far refused to every female child in the line. As she refused it to Betta for this child. And yet . . . and yet, it was not right to lock up the name forever. As each generation moved farther away from her own time, it and the happenings connected with it would then become more and more legendary, more and more unreal . . .

She put the matter for the thousandth time from her mind and turned back to buttoning up Fal Morgan. Passing down the long hall, she let her fingers trail for a second on its black wainscotting. Almost, she could feel a living warmth in the wood, the heart of the house beating. But there was nothing more she could do to protect it now. In the days to come, it, too, must take its chances.

Fifteen minutes later, she was on her own skimmer, headed downslope toward Foralie Town. At her back was an overnight bag, considerably smaller than the one they had packed for Betta. Under her belt was a heavy energy pistol on full charge and in perfect order. In the long-arm boot of the skimmer was an ancient blunderbus of a pellet shotgun, its clean and decent barrel replaced minutes before by one that was rusted and old, but workable. As she reached the foot of the slope and started the rise to the ridge, her gaze was filled by the mountains and Fal Morgan moved for the moment into the back of her mind.

The skimmer hummed upslope, only a few feet above the ground. Out from under the spruce and pine, the highland sun was brilliant. The thin earth cover, broken by outcroppings of granite and quartz was brown, sparsely covered by tough green grasses. The air was cold and light, yet unwarmed by the sun. She felt it deep in her lungs when she breathed. *The wine of the morning*, her own mother had called air like this, nearly a century ago.

She mounted to the crest of the ridge and the mountains stood up around her on all sides, shoulder to shoulder like friendly giants, as she topped the ridge and headed down the further slope to Foralie, now visible, distant and small by the river bend, far below. The sky was brilliantly clear with the new day. Only a small, stray cloud, here and there, graced its perfection. The mountains stood, looking down. There were people here who were put off by their bare rock, their remote and icy summits, but she herself found them honest – secure, strong and holding, brothers to her soul.

A deep feeling moved in her, even after all these years. Even more than for the home she had raised, she had found in herself a love for this world. She loved it as she loved her children, her children's children and her three husbands – each different, each unmatchable in its own way.

She had loved it, not more, but as much as she had loved her first-born, Jimmy, all the days of his life. But why should she love the Dorsai so much? There had been mountains in Wales – fine mountains. But when she had first come here after her second husband's death, something about this land, this planet, had spoken to her and claimed her with a voice different from any she had ever heard before. She and it had strangely become joined, beyond separation. A strange, powerful, almost aching affection had come to bind her to it. Why should just a world, a place of ordinary water and land and wind and sky, be something to touch her so deeply?

But she was sliding swiftly now, down the gentler, longer curve of the slope that led to Foralie Town. She could see the brown track of the river road, now, following the snake of blue water that wound away to the east and out between a fold in the mountains, and in its other direction from the town, west and up until it disappeared in the rocky folds above, where its source lay in the water of permanent ice sheets at seventeen thousand feet. Small clumps of the native softwood trees moved and passed like shutters between her and sight of the town below as she descended. But at this hour she saw no other traffic about. Twenty minutes later, she came to the road and the river below the town, and turned left, up-stream toward the buildings that were now close.

She passed out from behind a clump of small softwoods and slid past the town manufactory and the town dump, which now separated her from the river and the wharf that let river traffic unload directly to the manufactory. The manufactory itself was silent and inactive, at this early hour. The early sun winked on the rubble of refuse, broken metal and discarded material of all kinds, in the little hollow below the exhaust vent of the manufactory's power unit.

The Dorsai was a poor world in terms of arable land and most natural resources; but it did supply petroleum products from the drowned shorelines of the many islands that took the place of continents on the watery planet. So crude oil had been the fuel chosen for the power generator at the manufactory, which had been imported at great cost from Earth. The tools driven by that generator were as sophisticated as any found on Earth, while the dump was as primitive as any that pioneer towns had ever had. Like her Fal Morgan and the communications equipment within its wall.

She stopped the skimmer and got off, walking a dozen feet or so back into the brush across the road from the dump. She took the heavy energy handgun from her belt and hung it low on the branch of a sapling, where the green leaves all about would hide it from anyone not standing within arm's reach of it. She made no further effort to protect it. The broad arrow stamped on its grip, mark of the ap Morgans, would identify it to anyone native to this world who might stumble across it.

She returned to the skimmer, just as a metal door in the side of the manufactory slid back with a rattle and a bang. Jhanis Bins came out, wheeling a dump carrier loaded with silvery drifts of fine metallic dust.

Amanda walked over to him as he wheeled the carrier to the dump and tilted its contents onto the rubble inches below the exhaust vent. He jerked the carrier back on to the roadway and winked at Amanda. Age and illness had wasted him to a near skeleton, but there was still strength in his body, if little endurance. Above the old knife-scar laying all the way across his eyes held a sardonic humor.

'Nickel grindings?' asked Amanda, nodding at what Jhanis had just dumped.

'Right,' he said. There was grim humor in his voice as well as his eyes. 'You're up early.'

'So are you,' she said.

'Lots to be done.' He offered a hand. 'Amanda.'

She took it.

'Jhanis.'

He let go and grinned again.

'Well, back to work. Luck Commander, ma'm.'

He turned the carrier back toward the manufactory.

'News travels fast,' she said.

'How else?' he replied, over his shoulder, and went inside. The metal door rolled on its tracks, slamming shut behind him.

Amanda remounted the skimmer and slid it on into town. As she came to a street of houses just off the main street, she saw Bhaktabahadur Rais, sweeping the path between the flowers in front of his house, holding the broom awkwardly but firmly in the clawed arthritic fingers of the one hand remaining to him. The empty sleeve

24

of the other arm was pinned up neatly just below the shoulder joint. The small brown man smiled warmly as the skimmer settled to the ground when Amanda stopped its motor opposite him. He was no bigger than a twelve-year-old boy, but in spite of having almost as many years as Amanda, he moved as lightly as a child.

He carried the broom to the skimmer, leaned it against his shoulder and saluted. There was an impish sparkle about him.

'All right, Bhak,' said Amanda. 'I'm just doing what I'm asked. Did the young ones and their Ancients get out of town?'

He sobered.

'Piers sent them out two days ago,' he said. 'You didn't know?'

Amanda shook her head.

'I've been busy with Betta. Why two days ago?'

'Evidence they were out before we heard any Earth troops were coming.' He shifted his broom back into his hand. 'If nothing had happened it would have been easy to have called them back after a few days. If you need me for anything, Amanda –'

'I'll ask, don't worry,' she said. It would be easier at any time for Bhak to fight, than wait. The kukri in its curved sheath still lay on his mantelpiece. 'I've got to get on to the town hall.'

She lifted the skimmer on the thrust of its fans. Their humming was loud in the quiet street.

'Where's Betta?' Bhak raised his voice.

'Foralie.'

He smiled again.

'Good. Any news of Cletus?'

She shook her head and set the skimmer off down the street. Turning on to the main street, past the last house around the corner, she checked suddenly and went back. A heavy-bodied girl with long brown hair and a round somewhat bunched-up face was sitting on her front-step. Amanda stopped the skimmer, got out and went up to the

25

steps. The girl looked up at her.

'Marte,' said Amanda, 'what are you doing here? Why didn't you go out with the other boys and girls?'

Marte's face took on a slightly sullen look.

'I'm staying with grandma.'

'But you wanted to go with one of the teams,' said Amanda gently. 'You told me so just last week.'

Marte did not answer. She merely stared hard at the concrete of the walk between her feet. Amanda went up the steps past her and into the house.

'Berthe?' she called, as the door closed behind her.

'Amanda? I'm in the library.' The voice that came back was deep enough to be male, but when Amanda followed it into a room off to her right, the old friend she found among the crowded bookshelves there, seated at a desk, writing on a sheet of paper, was a woman with even more years than herself.

'Hello, Amanda,' Berthe Haugsrud said. 'I'm just writing some instructions.'

'Marte's still here,' Amanda said.

Berthe pushed back in her chair and sighed.

'It's her choice. She wants to stay. I can't bring myself to force her to go if she doesn't want to.'

'What have you told her?' Amanda heard the tone of her voice, sharper than she had intended.

'Nothing.' Berthe looked at her. 'You can't hide things from her, Amanda. She's as sensitive as . . . anyone. She picked it up – from the air, from the other young ones. Even if she doesn't understand details, she knows what's likely to happen.'

'She's young,' said Amanda. 'What is she – not seventeen yet?'

'But she's got no one but me,' said Berthe. Her eyes were black and direct under the wrinkled lids. 'Without me, she'd have nobody. Oh, I know everyone in town would look after her, as long as they could. But it wouldn't be the same. Here, in this house, with just the two of us, she can forget she's different. She can pretend she's just as bright

26

as anyone. With that gone . . .'

They looked at each other for a moment.

'Well, it's your decision,' said Amanda, turning away.

'And hers, Amanda. And hers.'

'Yes. All right. Goodby, Berthe.'

'Goodby, Amanda. Good luck.'

'The same to you,' said Amanda, soberly. 'The same to you.'

She went out, touching Marte softly on the girl's bowed head as she went by. Marte did not stir or respond. Amanda remounted the skimmer and drove it around the further corner, down the main street to the square concrete box that was the town hall.

'Hello, Jenna,' she said, stepping into the outer office. 'I'm here to be sworn in.'

Jenna Chalk looked up from her desk behind the counter that bisected the front office. She was a pleasant, rusty-haired woman, small and in her mid-sixties, looking like anything in the universe but the ex-mercenary she once had been.

'Good,' she said. 'Piers has been waiting. I'll bring the papers and we'll go back –'

'Still here?' said Amanda. 'What's he doing waiting around?'

'He wanted to see you.' Jenna slid her hands into the two wrist-crutches leaning against her desk, and levered herself to her feet. Leaning on one crutch, she picked up the folder before her on her desk and turned, leading the way down the corridor behind the counter that led toward the back of the building and the other offices there. Amanda let herself through the swinging gate in the counter and caught up.

'How is he?' Amanda asked.

'Worn out – a little easier since the sun came up,' said Jenna, hobbling along. Her bones, over the years, had become so fragile that they shattered at a touch, and her legs had broken so many times now that it was almost a miracle that she could walk at all. 'I think he'll let himself risk some medication, after he sees you take over.'

'He didn't need to wait for me,' said Amanda. 'That was foolish.'

'It's his way,' said Jenna. 'The habits of seventy years don't change.'

She stopped and pushed open the door they had come up against. Together they entered and found the massive, ancient shape of Piers propped up in a high-backed chair behind the wide desk of his office.

'Piers,' said Amanda. 'You didn't need to wait. Go home.'

'I want to witness your signing-in,' said Piers. Talking was still difficult for him, but Amanda noted that his breathing did seem to have eased slightly with the sunrise, in common asthmatic fashion. 'Just in case the troops they drop here decide to check records.'

'All right,' said Amanda.

Jenna was already switching on the recording camera eye in the wall. They went through the ritual of signing papers and administering an oath to Amanda that gave her the official title of Mayor of Foralie Town, which would be a cover for her secret rank of district commander.

'Now, for God's sake, go home!' said Amanda to Piers when they were done. 'Take some of that medicine of yours and sleep.'

'I will,' said Piers. 'Thank you for this, Amanda. And good luck. My skimmer's out back. Could you help me to it?'

Amanda put one hand under the heavy old man's right elbow and helped him to his feet. The years had taken much of her physical strength, but she still knew how to concentrate what she had at the point needed. She piloted Piers out the back way and helped him into the seat of his skimmer.

'Can you get down, and take care of yourself by yourself, when you get home?' she asked.

'No trouble,' Piers grunted at her. He put the skimmer's

power on and it lifted. He glanced at her once more.

'Amanda.'

'Piers.' She laid a hand for a second on his shoulder.

'It's a good world, Amanda.'

'I know. I think so, too.'

'Goodby.'

'Goodby,' said Amanda; and watched the skimmer take him away.

She turned back into the town hall.

'Marte's still here,' she said to Jenna. 'I guess, we'll just have to let her stay, if that's what she wants.'

'It is,' said Jenna.

'Are there any others still around I don't know about?'

'No, the young ones are all gone – and their Ancients.'

'Have you got a map for me?'

Jenna reached into her folder and came out with a map of the country about Foralie Town, up into the mountains surrounding. Initials in red were scattered about it.

'Each team is under the initials of its Ancient,' Jenna said.

Amanda studied it.

'They're all out in position, now, then?'

Jenna nodded.

'And they're all armed?'

'With the best we had to give them,' Jenna said. She shook her head. 'I can't help it, Amanda. It's bad enough for us at our age, but to give our young people hand weapons and ask them to stop –'

'Do you know an alternative?' said Amanda.

Jenna shook her head again, silently.

'An aircraft's due to pick me up from the pad here in three-quarters of an hour,' Amanda said. 'I'll be checking the situation out around the town otherwise, between now and then. Just in case I don't get back here before we're hit, are you going to have any trouble convincing the invaders that I'm a Mayor and nothing more?'

Jenna snorted.

'I've been clerk in this town hall nine years –'

'All right,' said Amanda. 'I just wanted to put it in

29

words. If the troops they send in won't billet in town, try and get them to camp close in on the up-river side.'

'Of course,' said Jenna. 'I know. You don't have to tell me, Amanda. Anyway, there shouldn't be much trouble getting them there. It's a natural bivouac area.'

'Yes. All right, then,' Amanda said. 'Take care of yourself, too, Jenna.'

'We both better take care of ourselves,' said Jenna. 'Luck, Amanda.'

Amanda went out.

She was on the airpad, waiting, when a light, four-place gravity aircraft dropped suddenly out of the blue above and touched down lightly on the pad. A door swung open. She went forward, carrying her single piece of luggage and climbed in. The craft took off. Amanda found herself seated next to Geoff Harbor, district commander of North Point.

'You both know each other, don't you?' asked the pilot, looking back over his shoulder.

'For sixteen years,' said Geoff. 'Hello, Amanda.'

'Geoff,' she said. 'They bringing you in for this meeting, too? Are you all ready, up there at North Point?'

'Yes. All set,' he answered both questions, looking at her curiously above his narrow nose and wedge-shaped chin. He was only in his forties, but twenty years of living with the aftereffects of massive battle injuries had given his skin a waxy look. 'I was expecting Eachan.'

'Eachan was asked by Cletus Grahame to hold himself ready for something else,' said Amanda. 'Piers took charge and I just replaced him this morning.'

'Asthma getting him?'

'The pressure of all this thing pushed him into an attack, I think,' said Amanda. 'Have you met this Arvid Johnson, or the other one – Bill Athyer?'

'I've met Arvid,' said Geoff. 'He's what Cletus Grahame's now calling a "battle op" – a field tactician. Athyer's a strategist and they work as a team – but you must have heard all this.'

'Yes,' said Amanda. 'But what I want to know is some first-hand opinions on what they're like.'

'Arvid struck me as being damn capable,' said Geoff. 'If they work well together, then Bill Athyer can't be much less. And if Cletus put them in charge of the defense here . . . but you know Cletus, of course?'

'He's a neighbor,' said Amanda. 'I've met him a few times.'

'And you've got doubts about him, too?'

'No,' said Amanda. 'But we're trying to make bricks without straw. A handful of adults with a force of half-grown teenagers to knock down an assault force of first-line troops. Miracles are going to have to be routine, and nothing's so good we shouldn't worry about whether it's good enough.'

Geoff nodded.

A short while later they set down on the airpad outside the island government center at South Point. A lean, brown-skinned soldier wearing the collar tabs that showed Groupman's rank – one of the staff of a dozen or so combat-qualified Dorsai that Arvid Johnson and Bill Athyer had been allowed to keep for the defense of the planet – was waiting for them as they stepped out of the aircraft. He led them to a briefing room already half-full of district commanders from all over the island, then turned to the room at large.

'If you'll take seats –' he announced. The district commanders sorted themselves out on the folding chairs facing a platform at one end of the room. A minute or so later, two men came in and stepped up on the platform. One was Arvid Johnson. Seen at full-length he was a tower of a man, with blond hair that in this artificial light looked so pale it seemed almost invisible. The unconquerability of him radiated to the rest of them in the room. The man beside him was of about the same age, but small, with a heavy beak of a nose – what Amanda had learned to call a 'Norman nose', when she had been a little girl. His eyes swept the room like gun muzzles.

31

The small man, Amanda thought, must be Bill Athyer, the strategist. At first glance, Bill might have appeared not only unimpressive, but sour – but Amanda's swift and experienced perceptions picked up something vibrant and brilliant in him. Literally, without loosing whatever painful and inhibiting self-consciousness and self-doubt he had been born with, he must somewhere have picked up the inner fire that now shone through his unremarkable exterior. He was all flame within – and that flame made him a strange contrast to the cool, almost remote competence of Arvid.

'Sorry to spring this on you,' Arvid said, when both men were standing on the platform and facing the audience. 'But it seems, after all, we can't wait for the district commanders who aren't here yet. We've just had word that whoever's navigating the invasion ships is either extremely lucky or very good. He's brought them out of their last phase shift right on top of the planet. They're in orbit overhead now and already dropping troops on our population centers.'

He paused and looked around the room.

'The rest of the Dorsai's been notified, of course,' he said. 'Bill Athyer and myself, with the few line soldiers we've got, are going to have to start moving – and keep moving. Don't try to find us – we'll find you. Communication will be known-person to known-person. In short, if the word you get from us doesn't come through somebody you trust implicitly, disregard it.'

'This is one of our strengths,' said Bill Athyer, so swiftly, it was almost as if he interrupted. His voice was harsh, but crackled with something like high excitement. 'Just as we know the terrain, we know each other. These two things let us dispense with a lot the invader has to have. But be warned – our advantages are going to be of most use only during the first few days. As they get to know us, they'll begin to be able to guess what we can do. Now, you've each submitted operational plans for the defense of your particular district within the general guidelines Arvid and I drew up. We've reviewed these plans, and by now you've all seen our recommendations for amendments and additions. If, in any case, there's more to be said, we'll get in touch with you as necessary. So you'd probably all better head back to your districts as quickly as possible. We've enough aircraft waiting to get you all back – hopefully before the invasion forces hit your districts. Get moving – is Amanda Morgan here?'

'Here!' called Amanda.

'Would you step up here, please?'

With Bill Athyer's last words, all the seated commanders had gotten to their feet, and she was hidden in the swarm of bodies. She pushed her way forward to the platform and looked up into the faces of the unusual pair standing there.

'I'm Amanda Morgan,' she said.

'A word with you before you leave,' said Bill. 'Will you come along?'

He led the way out of the briefing room. Arvid and Amanda followed. They stepped into a small office and Arvid shut the door behind them on the noise in the hall, as the other commanders moved to their waiting aircraft.

'You took command of the Foralie District just this morning,' Bill said. 'Have you had any chance to look at the plans handed in by the man you replaced?'

'Piers van der Lin checked with several of us when he drafted them,' Amanda said. 'But in any case, anyone in Foralie District over the age of nine knows how we're going to deal with whoever they send against us.'

'All right,' said Bill. Arvid nodded.

'You understand,' Bill went on. 'In Foralie, there, you'll be at the pick-point for whatever's going to happen. You can probably expect, if our information's right, to see Dow deCastries himself, as well as extra troops and a rank-heavier staff of enemy officers than any of the other districts. They'll be zeroing in on Foralie homestead.'

The thought of Betta and the unborn child there was a sudden twinge in Amanda's chest.

'There's no one at Foralie but Melissa Grahame and Eachan Khan, right now,' she said. 'Nobody to speak of.'

'There's going to be. Cletus will be on his way back as soon as the information we're invaded hits the Exotics – and I think you know the Exotics get news faster than anyone else. He may be on his way right now. Dow deCastries will be expecting this. So you can also expect your district to be one of the first, if not the first, hit. Odds are good that you, at least, aren't going to get home before the first troops touch down in your district. But we'll do our best for you. We've got our fastest aircraft holding for you now. Any last questions, or needs?'

Amanda looked at them both. Young men both of them.

'Not now,' she said. 'In any case, we know what we have to do.'

'Good.' It was Arvid speaking again. 'You'd better get going, then.'

The craft they were holding for her turned out to be a small, two-place high altitude gravity flyer, which rocketed to the ten-kilometer altitude, then back down toward Foralie on a flight path like the trajectory of a fired mortar shell. They were less than half an hour in the air. Nonetheless, as they plunged toward Foralie Town airpad, the com system inside the craft crackled.

Identify yourself. Identify yourself. This is Out-post Four-nine-three, Alliance-Coalition Expeditionary Force to the Dorsai. You are under our weapons. Identify yourself.

The pilot glanced briefly at Amanda and touched the transmit button on his control wheel.

'What'd you say?' he asked. 'This is Mike Amery, on a taxi run from South Point just to bring the Foralie Town Mayor home. Who did you say you were?'

Outpost Four-nine-three, Alliance-Coalition Expeditionary Force to the Dorsai. Identify the person you call the Mayor of Foralie Town.

'Amanda Morgan,' said Amanda, clearly, to the com

equipment, 'of the household ap Morgan, Foralie District.'

'*Hold. Do not attempt to land until we check your iden-tification. Repeat. Hold. Do not attempt to land until given permission.*'

The speaker was abruptly silent again. The pilot checked the landing pattern for the craft. They waited. After several minutes the order came to bring themselves in.

Two transport-pale, obviously Earth-native, privates in Coalition uniforms were covering the aircraft hatch with cone rifles, as Amanda preceded the pilot out on to the pad. A thin, serious-faced young Coalition lieutenant motioned the two of them to a staff car.

'Where do you think you're taking us?' Amanda demanded. 'Who are you? What're you doing here, any-way?'

'It'll all be explained at your town hall, ma'm,' said the lieutenant. 'I'm sorry, but I'm not permitted to answer questions.'

He got into the staff car with them and tapped the driver on the shoulder. They drove to town, through streets empty of any human figures not in uniforms. With the emptiness of the streets was a stillness. On the north edge of the town, on the upslope of the meadow which Amanda had mentioned to Jenna, Amanda could glimpse beehive-shaped cantonment-huts of bubble plastic being blown into existence in orderly rows – and from this area alone came a sound, distant but real, of voices and activities. Amanda felt the prevailing wind from the south on the back of her neck, and scented the faint odors of the fresh riverwater and the dump, carried by it, although the manufactory itself was silent.

The staff car reached the town hall. The pilot was left in the outer office, but Amanda was ushered in past guards to the office that had been Piers', and was now hers. There, a large map of the district had been imaged on one wall and several officers of grades between major and brigadier general were standing about in a discussion that seemed very close to argument. Only one person in the room wore

35

civilian clothing, and this was a tall, slim man seated at Amanda's desk, tilted back in its chair, apparently absorbed in studying the map that was imaged.

He seemed oddly remote from the rest, isolated by position or authority and willing to concentrate on the map, leaving the officers to their talk. The expression on his face was thoughtful, abstract. Few men Amanda had met in her long life could have legitimately been called handsome, but this man was. His features were so regular as to approach unnaturalness. His dark hair was touched with grey only at the temples, and his high forehead seemed to shadow deep-set eyes, so dark that they appeared inherently unreadable. If it had not been for those eyes and an air of power that seemed to wrap him like light from some invisible source, he might have looked too pretty to be someone to reckon with. Watching him now, however, Amanda had few doubts as to his ability, or his identity.

'Sir –' began the lieutenant who had brought Amanda in; but the brigadier to whom he spoke, glancing up, interrupted him, speaking directly to Amanda.

'You're the Mayor, here? What were you doing away from the town? Where are all your townspeople –'

'General,' Amanda spoke slowly. She did not have to invent the anger behind her words. 'Don't ask me questions. I'll do the asking. Who're you? What made you think you could walk into this office without my permission? Where'd you come from? And what're you doing here, under arms, without getting authority, first – from the island authorities at South Point, and from us?'

'I think you understand all right –' began the General.

'I think I don't,' said Amanda. 'You're here illegally and I'm still waiting for an explanation – and an apology for pushing yourself into my office without leave.'

The brigadier's mouth tightened, and the skin wrinkled and puffed around his eyes.

'Foralie District's been occupied by the Coalition-Alliance authorities,' he said. 'That's all you need to know. Now, I want some answers –'

'I'll need a lot more of an explanation than that,' broke in Amanda. 'Neither the Alliance nor the Coalition, nor any Coalition-Alliance troops, have any right I know of to be below parking orbit. I want your authority for being here. I want to talk to your superior – and I want both those things now!'

'What kind of a farce do you think you're playing?' The words burst out of the brigadier. 'You're under occupation –'

'General,' said a voice from the desk, and every head in the room turned to the man who sat there. 'Perhaps I ought to talk to the Mayor.'

'Yes sir,' muttered the brigadier. The skin around his eyes was still puffy, his face darkened now with blood-gorged capillaries. 'Amanda Morgan, this is Dow deCastries, Supreme Commander of Alliance-Coalition forces.'

'I didn't imagine he could be anyone else,' said Amanda. She took a step that brought her to the outer edge of her desk, and looked across it at Dow.

'You're sitting in my chair,' she said.

Dow rose easily to his feet and stepped back, gesturing to the now-empty seat.

'Please . . .' he said.

'Just stay on your feet. That'll be good enough for now,' said Amanda. She made no move to sit down herself. 'You're responsible for this?'

'Yes, you could say I am.' Dow looked at her thoughtfully. 'General Amorine –' he spoke without looking away from Amanda – 'the Mayor and I probably had better talk things over privately.'

'Yes sir, if that's what you want.'

'It is. It is, indeed.' Now Dow did look at the brigadier, who stepped back.

'Of course, sir,' Amorine turned on the lieutenant who had brought Amanda in. 'You checked her for weapons, of course?'

'Sir . . . I –' The lieutenant was flustered. His stiff

37

embarrassment pleaded that you did not expect a woman Amanda's age to go armed.

'I don't think we need worry about that, General.' Dow's voice was still relaxed; but his eyes were steady on the brigadier.

'Of course, sir.' Amorine herded his officers out. The door closed behind them, leaving Amanda and Dow standing face to face.

'You're sure you won't sit down?' asked Dow.

'This isn't a social occasion,' said Amanda.

'No,' said Dow. 'Unfortunately, no it isn't. It's a serious situation, in which your whole planet has been placed under Alliance-Coalition control. Effectively, what you call the Dorsai no longer exists.'

'Hardly,' said Amanda.

'You have trouble believing that?' said Dow. 'I assure you –'

'I've no intention of believing it now, or later,' Amanda said. 'The Dorsai isn't this town. It isn't any number of towns just like it. It's not even the islands and the sea – it's the people.'

'Exactly,' said Dow, 'and the people are now under control of the Alliance-Coalition. You brought it on yourself, you know. You've squandered your ordinary defensive force on a dozen other worlds, and you've got nothing but non-combatants left here. In short, you're helpless. But that's not my concern. I'm not interested in your planet, or your people, as people. It's just necessary we make sure they aren't led astray again by another dangerous madman like Cletus Grahame.'

'Madman?' echoed Amanda, dryly.

Dow raised his eyebrows.

'Don't you think he was mad in thinking he could succeed against the two richest powers on the most powerful human world in existence?' He shook his head. 'But there's not much point in our arguing politics, is there? All I want is your cooperation.'

'Or else what?'

'I wasn't threatening,' Dow said mildly.

'Of course you were,' said Amanda. She held his eyes with her own for a long second. 'Do you know your Shakespeare?'

'I did once.'

'Near the end of *Macbeth*, when Macbeth himself hears a cry in the night that signals the death of Lady Macbeth,' Amanda said, 'he says *"there was a time my senses would have cool'd to hear a night-shriek . . ."* remember it? Well, that time passes for all of us, with the years. You'll probably have a few to go yet to find that out for yourself; but if and when you do you'll discover that eventually you outlive fear, just as you outlive a lot of other things. You can't bully me, you can't scare me – or anyone else in Foralie District with enough seniority to take my place.'

It was his turn now to consider her for a long moment without speaking.

'All right,' he said. 'I'll believe you. My only interest, as I say, is in arresting Cletus Grahame and taking him back to Earth with me.'

'You occupy a whole world just to arrest one man?' Amanda said.

'Please.' He held up one long hand. 'I thought we were going to talk straightforwardly with each other. I want Cletus. Is he on the Dorsai?'

'Not as far as I know.'

'Then I'll go to his home and wait for him to come to me,' said Dow. He glanced at the map. 'That'll be Foralie – the homestead marked there near your own Fal Morgan?'

'That's right.'

'Then I'll move up there, now. Meanwhile I want to know what the situation is here, clearly. Your able fighting men are all off planet. All right. But there's no one in this town who isn't crippled, sick, or over sixty. Where are all your healthy young women, your teenagers below military age, and anyone else who's effective?'

'Gone off out of town,' said Amanda.

Dow's black eyes seemed to deepen.

'That hardly seems normal. I assume you had warnings of us, at least as soon as we were in orbit. I'd be very surprised if it wasn't news of our being in orbit that brought you back here in that aircraft just now. You wouldn't have messaged ahead, telling your children and able-bodied adults to scatter and hide?'

'No,' said Amanda. 'I didn't; and no one here gave any such direction.'

'Then maybe you'll explain why they're all gone?'

'Do you want a few hundred reasons?' Amanda said. 'It's the end of summer. The men are gone. This town is just a supply and government center. Who's young and wants to hang around here all day? The younger women living in town are up visiting at the various homesteads where they've got friends and there's some social life. The babies and younger children went with their mothers. The older children are off on team exercises.'

'Team exercises?'

'Military team exercises,' said Amanda, bluntly and with grim humor, watching him. 'Otherwise known as "creeping and crawling". This is a world where the main occupation, once you're grown, is being a mercenary soldier. So this is our version of field trips. It's good exercise, the youngsters get some academic credit for it when they go back to school in a few weeks, and it's a chance for them to get away from adult supervision and move around on their own, camping out.'

Dow frowned.

'No adult supervision?'

'Not a lot,' said Amanda. 'There's one adult – called an "Ancient", with each team, in case of emergencies; but in most cases the team makes its own decision about what kind of games it'll play with other teams in the same area, where it'll set up camp, and so forth.'

'These children,' Dow was still frowning, 'are they armed?'

'With real weapons? They never have been.'

'Are they likely to get any wild notions about doing

something to our occupying forces –'

'Commander,' said Amanda, 'Dorsai children don't get wild notions about military operations. Not if they expect to stay Dorsai as adults.'

'I see,' said Dow. He smiled slowly at her. 'All the same, I think we better get them and the able-bodied adults back into town here, where we can explain to them what the situation is and what they should or shouldn't do. Also, there's a few of your other people who're conspicuous by their absence. For example, where are your medical people?'

'We've got one physician and three meds, here in Foralie District,' said Amanda. 'They all ride circuit most of the time. You'll find them scattered out at various homesteads, right now.'

'I see,' said Dow again. 'Well, I think you better call them in as well, along with any other adult from the homesteads who's physically able to come.'

'No,' said Amanda.

He looked at her. His eyebrows raised.

'Courage, Amanda Morgan,' he said, 'is one thing. Stupidity, something else.'

'And nonsense is nonsense wherever you find it,' said Amanda. 'I told you, you couldn't bully me – or anyone else you'll find in this town. And you'll need one of us who's here to deal with the people of the district for you. I can bring the youngsters back in if necessary, and with them such adults from the homesteads who don't need to stay where they are. If the medical people are free to come in, I can get them, too. But in return, I'll want some things from you.'

'I don't think you're in a position to bargain.'

'Of course I am,' said Amanda. 'Let's not play games. It's much easier for you if you can get civilian cooperation – it's much faster. Difficulty with the populace means expense, when you're carrying the cost of enough troops to nail down a planet – even as sparsely settled a planet as this one. And you yourself said once you get Cletus you'll

41

be taking off without another thought for the rest of us.'

'That's not exactly what I said,' Dow replied.

Amanda snorted.

'All right,' he said, 'what was it you had in mind?'

'First, get your troops out of our town unless you were thinking of billeting them in our homes, here?'

'I think you saw camp being set up just beyond the houses a street or two over.'

'All right,' Amanda said. 'Then I want them to stay out of town unless they've got actual business here. When they do come in, they're to come in as visitors, remembering their manners. I don't want any of your officers, like that brigadier just now, trying to throw their weight around. Our people are to be free of any authority from yours, so we can get back to business as usual – and that includes putting the manufactory back into operation, immediately. I noticed you'd had the power shut off. Don't you realize we've got contracts to fill – contracts for manufactured items, so that we can trade with the rest of Dorsai for the fish, the grain and other things we have to have to live?'

'All right,' said Dow. 'I suppose we can agree to those things.'

'I'm not finished,' Amanda said, swiftly. 'Also, you and all the rest of your forces are to stay put, in your encampment. I don't want you upsetting and alarming the district while I go find the teams and get people back here from the homesteads. It'll take me a week, anyway –'

'No,' said Dow. 'We'll be putting out patrols immediately; and I myself'll be leaving with an escort for Foralie homestead in a few hours.'

'In that case –' Amanda was beginning, but this time it was Dow who cut her short.

'In that case –' his voice was level, 'you'll force me to take the more difficult and time-consuming way with your people. I didn't bargain with you on any of the other things you asked for. I'm not bargaining now. Go ahead and take back your town, start up your manufactory, and round up only those you feel can come in safely. But our patrols go out as soon as we're ready to send them; and I leave, today, just as I said. Now, do we have an agreement?'

Amanda nodded, slowly.

'We have,' she said. 'All right, you'd better get those officers of yours back in here. I'm going to have to move to cover the district personally, even in a week. I'll go right now, but I want to hear that manufactory operating before I'm out of earshot of town. I suppose you've got Jhanis Bins closed up in his house, like everyone else.'

'Whoever he is,' said Dow. 'He'd be under house quarantine, yes.'

'All right, I'll call him,' said Amanda. 'But I want your General Amorine to send an officer to get him and take him safely to the manufactory, just in case some of your enlisted men may not have heard word of this agreement by that time.'

'Fair enough,' said Dow. He stepped to the desk and keyed the com system there. 'General, will you and your staff step back into the office, here?'

'Yes, Mr. deCastries.' The voice from the wall came promptly.

Twenty minutes later, Amanda reached the airpad in the same staff car that had brought her in from it. Under the eye of the two enlisted men on duty there, her skimmer stood waiting for her.

'Thanks,' she said to the young lieutenant who had brought her in. She climbed out of the staff car, walked across the pad and got into her skimmer.

'Just a minute,' called the lieutenant.

She looked back to see him standing up in his staff car. There was a shine to his forehead that told of perspiration.

'You've got a weapon there, ma'm,' he said. 'Just a minute. Soldier – you!' He pointed to one of the enlisted men guarding the pad. 'Get that piece and bring it over to me.'

'Lieutenant,' said Amanda, 'this is still a young planet and we had lawless people roaming around our mountains as recently as just a few years back. We all carry guns here.'

'Sorry, ma'm. I have to examine it. Soldier . . .'

The enlisted man came over to the skimmer, pulled the pellet shotgun from the scabbard beside her and winked at her.

'Got to watch you dangerous outworlders,' he said, under his breath. He glanced over the pellet gun, turned it up to squint down its barrel and chuckled, again under his breath.

He carried the weapon to the lieutenant, and said something Amanda could not catch. The lieutenant also tilted the pellet gun up to look briefly into its barrel, then handed it back.

'Take it to her,' he ordered. He lifted his head and called across to Amanda. 'Be careful with it, ma'm.'

'I will be,' said Amanda.

She received the rifle, powered up the skimmer and slid off through the fringe of trees around the pad.

She took her way toward the downriver side of town. As she went, the sudden throb of the engines in the manufactory erupted on her ear. She smiled, but she was suddenly conscious of the prevailing wind in her face. Sweating, she asked herself, at your age? She turned her scorn inward. What was all that talk of yours to deCastries about having outlived fear?

She swung through town and around by the river road past the dump. The manufactory stood, noisily operating. There was no Coalition uniform in sight outside the building and the side looking in her direction was blank of windows. She stopped her skimmer long enough to walk back into the brush and retrieve the energy handgun she had hung on the tree. Then she remounted her skimmer and headed upslope, out of town.

Her mind was racing. Dow had intimated he would head out to Foralie homestead yet this afternoon. Which meant Amanda herself would have to go directly there to get there before him. She had hoped to come in there with evening, and perhaps even stay overnight to see how Betta was doing. Now it would have to be a case of getting in and out in an hour at most. And, almost more important, either before or after she reached there, she had to reach the team which was holding the territory through which Dow and his escort would pass.

Who was Ancient for that team? So many things had happened so far this day that she had to search her memory for a moment before it came up with the name of Ramon Dye. Good. Ramon was one of the best of the Ancients; and, aside from the fact that he was legless, strong as a bull.

Thinking deeply, she slid the skimmer along under maximum power. She was burning up a month's normal expenditure of energy in a few days, with her present spend-thrift use of the vehicle; but there was a time for thriftiness and a time to spend. Of her two choices, it would have to be a decision to contact Ramon's team first, before going to Foralie. Ramon's team would have to send runners to the other teams, since even visual signals would be too risky, with the Coalition troops at Foralie town probably loaded with the latest in surveillance equipment. The more time she could give the runners, the better.

It was a stroke of bad luck, Dow's determination to send out patrols and go so immediately to Foralie himself. Bad on two counts. Patrols out meant some of the troops away from the immediate area of the town, at all times. It would have been much better to have them all concentrated there. Also, patrols out meant that sooner or later some of them would have to be taken care of by the teams – and that, while it would have to be faced if and when it came, was something not good to think about until then. There would be a heavy load thrown on the youngsters – not only to do what had to be done, but to do it with the coolheadedness and calculation of adults, without which they could not succeed, and their lives would be thrown away for nothing.

She reminded herself that up through medieval times, twelve- and fourteen-year-olds had been commonly found in armies. Ships' boys had been taken for granted in the navies of the eighteenth and nineteenth centuries. But these historical facts brought no comfort. The children who would be going up against Earth-made weapons here would be children she had known since their birth.

But she must not allow them to guess how she felt. Their faith in their seniors, well-placed or misplaced, was something they would need to hang on to as long as possible for their own sakes.

She came at last to a mountain meadow a full meter high with fall grass. The meadow was separated by just one ridge from Foralie homestead. Amanda turned her skimmer into the shade of a clump of native softwoods on the upslope edge of the meadow, below the ridge. On the relatively open ground beneath those trees she put the vehicle down and waited.

It was all of twenty minutes before her ear picked up – not exactly a sound that should not have been there, but a sound that was misplaced in the rhythm of natural noises surrounding her. She lifted her voice.

'All right!' she called. 'I'm in a hurry. Come on in!'

Heads emerged above the grasstops, as close as half a dozen meters from her and as far out as halfway across the meadow. Figures stood up; tanned, slim figures in flexible shoes, twill slacks strapped tight at the ankle and long-sleeved, tight-wristed shirts, all of neutral color. One of the tallest, a girl about fifteen, put two fingers in her mouth and whistled.

A skimmer came over the ridge and hummed down toward Amanda until it sank to a stop beside her on the ground. The team members, ranging in age from eight years of age to sixteen, were already gathering around the two of them.

Amanda waited until they were all there, then nodded to the man on the other skimmer and looked around the closed arc of sun-browned faces, sun-bleached hair.

'The invaders are here, in Foralie town,' she said. 'Coalition first-line troops under a brigadier and staff, with Dow deCastries.'

The faces looked back at her in silence. Adults would have reacted with voice and feature. These looked at her with the same expressions they had shown before; but Amanda, knowing them all, could feel the impact of the news on them.

'Everyone's out?' the man on the other skimmer asked.

Amanda turned again to the Ancient. Perched on his skimmer the way he was, Ramon Dye might have forced a stranger to look twice before discovering that there were no legs below Ramon's hips. Strapped openly in the boot of his vehicle, behind him, were the two artificial legs he normally used in town; but out here, like the team members, he was stripped to essentials. His square, quiet face under its straight brown hair looked at her with concern.

'Everybody's out but those who're supposed to be there,' said Amanda. 'Except for Marte Haugsrud. She decided to stay with her grandmother.'

Still, there was that utter silence from the circle of faces, although more than half a dozen of them had grown up within a few doors of Berthe. It was not that they did not feel, Amanda reminded herself; it was that by instinct, like small animals, they were dumb under the whiplash of fate.

'But we've other things to talk about,' she said – and felt the emotion she had evoked in them with her news, relax under the pressure of her need for their attention. 'DeCastries is taking an armed escort with him to Foralie to wait for Cletus; and he's also going to start sending out patrols, immediately.'

She looked about at them all.

'I want you to get runners out to the nearest other teams – nothing but runners, mind you, those troops will be watching for any recordable signalling – and tell them to pass other runners on to spread the word. Until you get further word from me, all patrols are to be left alone; completely alone, no matter what they do. Watch them, learn everything you can about them, but stay out of sight. Pass that word on to the homesteads, as well as to the other teams.'

47

She paused, looking around, waiting for questions. None came.

'I've made an agreement with deCastries that I'll bring all the teams and all the able adults in from the homesteads to Foralie Town, to be told the rules of the occupation. I've told him it'll take me at least a week to round everyone up. So we've got that much time, anyway.'

'What if Cletus doesn't come home in a week?' asked the girl who had whistled for Ramon.

'Cross that bridge when we come to it,' said Amanda. 'But I think he'll be here. Whether he is or not, though, we've still got the district to defend. Word or order from Arvid Johnson and Bill Athyer is to be trusted only if it comes through someone you trust personally – pass that along to the other teams and homesteads, too. Now, I'm going on up to Foralie to brief them on Dow's coming. Any questions or comments, so far?'

'Betta hasn't had her baby yet,' said a young voice.

'Thanks for telling me,' said Amanda. She searched the circle with her eyes, but she was not able to identify the one who had just spoken. 'Let's stick to business for the moment, though. I've got a special job for your best infiltrator – unless one of the neighboring teams has someone better than you have. Have they?'

Several voices told her immediately that the others had not.

'Who've you got, then?'

'Lexy –' the voices answered.

An almost white-haired twelve-year old girl was pushed forward, scowling a little. Amanda looked at her – Alexandra Andrea, from Tormai homestead. Lexy, like the others, was slim by right of youth; but a squareness of shoulder and a sturdiness of frame were already evident. For no particular reason, Amanda suddenly remembered how her own hair, as a child, had been so blond as to be almost white.

The memory of her young self brought another concern to mind. She looked searchingly at Lexy. What she knew about Lexy included indications of a certain amount of independence and a flair for risk-taking. Even now, obviously uncomfortable at being shoved forward this way, Lexy was still broadcasting an impression of truculence and self-acknowledged ability. Character traits, Amanda thought, remembering her own childhood again, that could lead to a disregard of orders and to chance-taking.

'I need someone to go in close to the cantonments the occupation troops have set up at Foralie Town,' she said aloud. 'Someone who can listen, pick up information, and get back with it safely. Note – I said safely.'

She locked eyes with Lexy.

'Do you take chances, Lexy?' she asked. 'Can I trust you to get in and get out without taking risks?'

There was a sudden outbreak of hoots and laughter from the team.

'Send Tim with her!'

Lexy flushed. A slight boy, Lexy's age or possibly as much as a year or two younger, was pushed forward. Beside Lexy, he looked like a feather beside a rock.

'Timothy Royce,' Amanda said, looking at him. 'How good are you, Tim?'

'He's good,' said Lexy. 'That is, he's better than the rest of these elephants.'

'Lexy won't take chances with Tim along,' said the girl who had whistled. Amanda was vainly searching her memory for this one's name. Sometimes when they shot up suddenly, she lost track of who they were; and the tall girl was already effectively an adult.

'How about it, Tim?' Amanda asked the boy. Tim hesitated.

'He gets scared,' a very young voice volunteered.

'No, he doesn't!' Lexy turned on the crowd. 'He's cautious, that's all.'

'No,' said Tim, unexpectedly. 'I do get scared. But with Lexy I can do anything you want.'

He looked openly at Amanda.

Amanda looked at Ramon.

'I can't add anything,' he said, shaking his head. 'Lexy's good, and Tim's pretty good – and they work well together.'

His eyes settled on Amanda's suddenly.

'But do you have to have someone from one of the teams?'

'Who else is there?'

'One of the older ones, then . . .' his voice trailed off. Amanda looked back at the faces ringed about.

'Team?' she asked.

There was a moment of almost awkward silence and then the girl who had whistled – Leah Abo, the name suddenly leaped into existence in Amanda's mind – spoke.

'Any of us'll go,' she said. 'But Lexy's the best.'

'That's it, then,' said Amanda. She put the power to her skimmer, and lifted it off the ground. 'Lexy, Tim – I'll meet you after dark tonight, just behind the closest ridge above the meadow north of town. All of you – be careful. Don't let the patrols see you. And get those runners out as fast as you can.'

She left them, the circle parted and she hummed up and over the ridge. Foralie homestead lay on a small level space a couple of hundred meters beyond her, on a rise that commanded a clear view in all directions as far as the town itself.

Behind the long, low, timbered house there, she could see the oversize jungle gym that Cletus had caused to be constructed at Grahame-House and then moved here, after his marriage to Melissa. It had been a device to help him build himself back physically after his knee operation, and there was no reason for it to evoke any particular feeling in her. But now, seeing its spidery and intricate structure casting its shadow on the roof of the long, plain-timbered house beneath it, she suddenly felt – almost as if she touched the cold metal of it with her hand – the hard, intricately woven realities that would be bringing Dow and Cletus to their final meeting beneath that shadow.

She slid the skimmer down to the house. Melissa, with the tall, gray-mustached figure of Eachan Khan beside her, came out of the front door; and they were standing, waiting for her as she brought the skimmer up to them and dropped it to the ground.

'Betta's fine, Amanda,' said Melissa. 'Still waiting. What's going on?'

'The occupation troops are down in Foralie Town.'

'We know,' said Eachan Khan, in his brief, clipped British-accented speech. 'Watched them drop in, using the scope on our roof.'

'They've got Dow deCastries with them,' Amanda said, getting down from the skimmer. 'He's after Cletus, of course. He plans to come up here to Foralie right away. He may be right behind me –'

The ground under her feet seemed to rock suddenly. She found Eachan Khan holding her up.

'Amanda!' said Melissa, supporting her on the other side. 'When did you eat last?'

'I don't rememb . . .' she found the words had difficulty coming out. Her knees trembled, and she felt close to fainting. A distant fury filled her. This was the aspect of her age that she resented most deeply. Rested and nourished, she could face down a deCastries. But let any unusual time pass without food and rest and she became just another frail oldster.

Her next awareness was of being propped up on a couch in the Foralie sitting room, with a pillow behind her back. Melissa was helping her sip hot, sweet tea with the fiery taste of Dorsai whisky in it. Her head began to clear. By the time the cup was empty, there was a plate of neatly cut sandwiches made by Eachan Khan, on the coffee table beside her. She had forgotten how delicious sandwiches could be.

'What's the rest of the news, then?' Eachan asked, when she had eaten. 'What happened to you today?'

She told them.

'. . . I must admit, Eachan,' she said, as she wound up, looking at the stiff-backed ex-general, 'I wasn't too pleased about Cletus asking you to sit on your hands, here – and even less pleased with you for agreeing. But I think I

51

understand it better since I met deCastries, himself. If any one of them's likely to suspect how we might defend ourselves, it'll be him, not those officers with him. And the one thing that'll go farther to keep him from starting to suspect anything, will be finding you puttering around here, keeping house right under his nose while he waits for Cletus. He knows your military reputation.'

'Wouldn't call it puttering,' said Eachan. 'But you're right. Cletus does have a tendency to think around corners.'

'Let alone the fact –' Amanda held his eye with her own, 'that if something happens to me, you'll still be here to take over.'

'Depends on circumstance.'

'Nonetheless,' said Amanda.

'Of course,' Eachan said. 'Naturally, if I'm free – and needed – I'd be available.'

'Yes –' Amanda broke off suddenly. 'But I've got to get out of here!'

She sat up abruptly on the couch, swinging her feet to the floor.

'DeCastries and his escort are probably right behind me. I'd just planned to drop by and brief you –'

She got to her feet, but lightheadedness took her again at the sudden movement and she sat down again, unexpectedly.

'Amanda, be sensible. You can't go anywhere until you've rested for a few hours,' said Melissa.

'I tell you, deCastries –'

'Said he'd be up here yet today? I don't think so,' said Eachan.

She turned, almost to glare at him.

'What makes you so sure?'

'Because he's no soldier. Bright of course – Lord yes, he's bright. But he's not a soldier. That means he's in the hands of those officers of his. Earth-bound types, still thinking in terms of large-unit movements. They might get patrols out, late in the day, but they won't get Dow off.'

'What if he simply orders them to get him off?' Amanda demanded.

'They'll promise him, of course, but somehow everybody won't be together, the vehicles won't be set, with everything harnessed up and ready to go, before sundown; and even Dow'll see the sense of not striking out into unfamiliar territory with night coming on.'

'How can you be that sure?' Melissa asked her father.

'That brigadier's got his own future to think of. Better to have Dow down on him over not getting off on time than to send someone like Dow out and turn out to be the officer who lost him. The day's more than half over. If Dow and his escort get bogged down for even a few hours by some harebrained locals fighting back – that's the way the brigadier'll be thinking – they could end up being caught out, unable to move, in the open at dark. Strange country, nighttime, and an open perimeter's chancy with a prize political package like Dow. No, no – he won't be here until tomorrow at the earliest.'

Eachan cocked an eye on Amanda.

'But if you like,' he said, 'Melly and I'll take turns on the scope up on the roof. If anything moves out of Foralie we can see it; and by the time we're sure it's definitely moving in this direction, we'll still have two hours before it can get here at column speed. Take a nap, Amanda. We'll call you if you need to move.'

Amanda gave in. Stretched out on a large bed in one of the wide, airy bedrooms of Foralie, the curtains drawn against the sunlight, she fell into a heavy sleep from which she roused, it seemed, within minutes. But, blinking the numbness of slumber from her vision, she saw that beyond the closed curtains there was now darkness, and the room around her was plunged in a deeper gloom than that of curtained daylight.

'What time is it?' she called out, throwing back the single blanket with which she had been covered. No answer came. She sat on the edge of the bed, summoning herself to awareness, then got to her feet and let herself out into the

53

hall, where artificial lights were lit.

'What time is it?' she repeated, coming into the kitchen. Both Eachan Khan and Melissa looked up from the table there, and Melissa got to her feet.

'Two hours after sunset,' she answered. But Amanda had already focused on the wall clock across the room, which displayed the figure 21:10. 'Sit down, Amanda. You'll want some tea.'

'No,' said Amanda. 'I was supposed to meet two of the youngsters from the local team just above Foralie Town before sunset –'

'We know,' said Eachan. 'We had a runner from that team when they saw you didn't leave here. The two you're talking about went, and Ramon went with them. He knows what you want in the way of information.'

'I've got to get down there, to meet them.'

'Amanda – sit!' said Melissa from the kitchen unit. 'Tea'll be ready for you in a second.'

'I don't want any tea,' said Amanda.

'Of course you do,' said Melissa.

Of course she did. It was another of her weaknesses of age. She could almost taste the tea in anticipation, and her sleep-heavy body yearned for the internal warmth that would help it wake up. She sat down at the table opposite Eachan.

'Fine watch you keep,' she said to him.

'Nothing came from Foralie Town in this direction before sunset,' he said. 'They're not starting out with Dow in the dark, as I said. So I came back inside, of course. You could stay the night, if you want.'

'No, I've got to get there; and I've a lot of ground to cover –' she broke off as Melissa placed a steaming cup before her. 'Thanks, Melissa.'

'But why don't you stay the night?' Melissa asked, sitting back down at the table, herself. 'Betta's already asleep, but you could see her in the morning –'

'No. I've got to go.'

Melissa looked at her father.

'Dad?'

'No,' said Eachan, 'I think perhaps she's right. But will you come back for the night afterwards, Amanda?'

'No. I don't know where I'll light.'

'If you change your mind,' said Melissa. 'Just come to the door and ring. But I don't have to tell you that.'

Amanda left Foralie homestead half an hour later. The moon, which had been full the night before, was just past full, but scattered clouds cut down the brilliant night illumination she had woken to early that morning. She made good time on the skimmer toward the ridge where she had arranged to meet Lexy and Tim. A hundred meters or so behind it, she found Ramon's skimmer, empty, and dropped her own beside it. No one was in sight. Ramon could not walk upright without his prosthetics, but he could creep-and-crawl as well as any other adult. Amanda was about to work her way up to the ridge, herself, staying low so that any instruments in the cantonment below would not discover her, when a rustle in the shadows warned her of people returning. A few moments later, Ramon, Lexy and Tim all rose from the ground at arms-length from her.

'Sorry,' said Amanda, 'I should have been here earlier.'

'It wasn't necessary,' said Ramon. His powerful arms hauled him up on to his own skimmer and he sat upright there.

'Yes, it was,' said Amanda. 'You didn't let these two go in until things were shut down –'

'They didn't go down until full dark,' said Ramon. 'Not until the last of the patrols had left and the manufactory was shut down. The townsfolk were all inside and the troops were all in their cantonment area. Tim stayed beyond the perimeter there and Lexy went up to just outside the outer line of huts, close enough so she could hear them talking, but with plenty of room to leave if she needed to.'

Amanda transferred her attention to Lexy.

'What were they talking about?'

'Usual stuff,' said Lexy. 'The officers, and the equipment, how long they'd be here before they'd ship off again. Regular soldier off-duty talk.'

'Did they talk about when deCastries would be leaving for Foralie?'

'First thing in the morning. They'd stalled about getting ready, so he couldn't get off today,' said Lexy. 'They don't think much of those of our people who're left here; but still none of them I heard talking felt much like starting out with night coming on.'

'What do they think of their officers?'

'Nothing great. There's a major they all like, but he's not on the general's staff. They really draw the line between enlisted and officer.'

'Now, you see for yourself, how that is with Old World troops,' commented Ramon to the two young ones.

'It's a pretty stupid way for them to be, all the same, out here in hostile territory,' said Lexy. 'But they've got a good pool of light vehicles. No armor. Vehicle-mounted light weapons and handweapons. I could have brought you one of their cone rifles –'

'Oh, could you?'

There was a little silence in the darkness, that betrayed Lexy's recognition of her slip of the tongue.

'The whole line of huts was empty. All I did was look in the last one in the line,' said Lexy. 'These Earth troops – they're worse than elephants. I could have gone in and picked their pockets and got out without their knowing about it.'

The moon came from behind a cloud that had been hiding it, and in the pale light Amanda could see Lexy's face . . . tightmouthed.

'Ramon,' said Amanda. 'Didn't you tell them specifically not to go into the cantonment area?'

'I'm sorry, Amanda,' said Ramon. 'I didn't. Not specifically.'

'Lexy, under no conditions, now or in the future, do you or anyone else go beyond the outer line of huts.' Exasperation took her suddenly. 'And don't bristle! If you have to resent an order, try to keep the fact to yourself.'

Another cloud obscured the moon. Lexy's voice came unexpectedly out of the darkness.

'Why?'

'For one reason, because an hour later you may wish you had. For another, learn never to challenge automatically. No one's that good. Sit on your impulse until you know everything that's likely to happen when you act on it.'

Silence out of the darkness. Amanda wondered whether Lexy was filing the information she had just received in the automatic discard file of her mind, or – just possibly – tucking it away for future reference.

'Now,' Amanda said. 'Anything else? Any talk of plans? Any talk of Cletus being on the way here?'

'No,' said Lexy. 'They did talk about relocation, after Cletus is tried back on Earth. And they even said something about changing the name of our planet. That doesn't make sense.'

Amanda breathed deeply.

'I'm afraid it does,' she said.

'Amanda?' It was Ramon asking. 'I'm not sure I follow you.'

'DeCastries tried to give me the impression that this whole invasion was designed only to arrest Cletus and take him back to Earth to stand trial. I let him think I went along with that. But of course they've got a lot more than that in mind, with the expense they've gone to here. What they really want to do is bury the Dorsai – and everyone in uniform wearing that name. Obviously what they've planned is to use Cletus' trial as a means to whip up Earth sentiment. Then, with a lot of public backing, they can raise the funds they'd need to spread our people out on other worlds, and give this world a new name and a new breed of settler.'

Amanda thought for a moment, while the moon continued to play peekaboo with the clouds.

'I'd better go back to Foralie tonight, after all,' she said.

'Eachan will have to know this, in case he has to take over. Lexy – anything else?'

'Nothing, Amanda, really. Just off-duty talk.'

'All right. I want this listening to go on – only at night, though, after the town and the cantonment's settled down. Ramon, will you stay on top of that? And also make sure neither Lexy or anyone else goes into the cantonment area. Past the outer line sentries is all right, if they know what they're doing. But not, repeat not, into the cantonment streets; and never into the huts, themselves. There's more here than just your personal risk to think about, Lexy. It's our whole world, and all of us, at stake.'

Silence.

'All right, Amanda, we'll take care of it,' said Ramon. 'And we'll get word to you if anything breaks.'

'The necessary thing,' said Amanda, 'is letting me know if there's any word of Cletus getting here. All right. I'll see you tomorrow evening.'

She lifted her skimmer on minimum power to keep the sound of its motors down and swung away in the direction of Foralie. Had she been unfairly hard on Lexy? The thought walked through her mind, unbidden. It was not an unfamiliar thought, nowadays; Betta, Melissa, Lexy . . . a number of them evoked it in her. How far was she justified in expecting them to react as she, herself, would? To what extent was it right of her to expect a future Amanda to react as she would?

No easy answer came to her. On the surface it was unfair. She was unfair. On the other hand there were the inescapable facts. There was the need that someone, at least, react as she did; and the reality that what she required of them was what experience had taught her life required of them all. Forcibly, she put the unresolved problem once again from her; and made herself concentrate on the imperative of the moment.

Mid-morning of the following day she lay in tall grass, high on a slope, and watched the train that was the escort of Dow deCastries, winding up through the folds of the hills toward Foralie. Around her were the members of Ramon's team. The train consisted of what looked like two platoons of enlisted men, under four officers and Dow himself, all sliding over the ground in air-cushion staff cars, with a heavy energy rifle deck-mounted on every car but the one occupied by Dow. The vehicles moved with the slowness of prudence, and there were flankers out on skimmers, as well as two skimmers at point.

'They'll reach Foralie in another twenty minutes or so,' Ramon said in Amanda's ear. 'What should we do about getting runners in to Eachan and Melissa?'

'Don't send anyone in,' Amanda said. 'Eachan will come out to you if he wants contact. Or maybe Melissa will. At any rate, let them set it up. Tell them I've gone to look at the situation generally throughout the district. I need to know what the other patrols sent out are doing.'

She waited until the train had disappeared over the ridge toward which it had been heading, then slid back down into the small slope behind her, where her skimmer was hidden.

'You're fully powered?' asked Ramon, looking at the skimmer.

'Enough for non-stop operation for a week,' said Amanda. 'I'll see you this evening, down above the cantonments.'

The rest of that day she was continually on the move. It was quite true, as she had told Dow, that it would take her a week to fully cover the homesteads of the Foralie district. But it was not necessary for what she had in mind to call at every homestead, since she had a communications network involving the teams and the people in the homesteads themselves. She needed only to call at those few homesteads where she needed personal contact with such as the medical personnel or such as Tosca Aras, invalided home and anchored in his house by age and a broken leg. Tosca, like Eachan, was an experienced tactical mind to whom the rest could turn in case anything took her out of action.

In any case, her main interest was in the patrols Dow had sent out. Eachan, watching with the scope on the Foralie rooftop, reported two had gone out the evening before and this morning another four had taken their way on different bearings, out into the district. In each case they seemed to be following a route taking them to the homesteads of a certain area of the district on a swing that looked like it might last twenty-four hours, and at the end of that time bring them back to Foralie Town and their cantonments.

'They don't seem to be out looking for trouble,' Myron Lee, Ancient for one of the other teams, said to Amanda as they stood behind a thicket, looking down on one of these patrols. Myron, lean to the point of emaciation and in his fifties, was hardly any stronger physically than Amanda, but radiated an impression of unconquerable energy.

'On the other hand,' he went on, 'they didn't exactly come out unprepared for trouble, either.'

The patrol they were watching, like all the others Amanda had checked, was a single platoon under a single commissioned officer. But its personnel were mounted on staff cars and skimmers, as the escort for Dow had been; and in this case, every staff car mounted a heavy energy rifle, while the soldiers riding both these and the skimmers carried both issue cone rifles and sidearms.

'What have they been doing when they reach a homestead?' Amanda asked.

'They take the names and images of the people there, and take images of the homestead, itself. Census work, of a sort,' said Myron.

Amanda nodded. She had been given the same description whenever she had asked that question about other patrols. It was not unusual military procedure to gather data about the people and structures in any area where a force was stationed – but the method of the particular survey seemed to imply that the people and buildings surveyed might need to be taken by force, at some time in the future.

By evening she was back behind the ridge over-looking the meadow holding the cantonments. Lexy, Tim and Ramon had been waiting when she got there. They waited a little longer, together, while twilight gave way to full dark. The clouds were even thicker this night; and when the last of the light was gone, they could not see each other; even at arm's length.

'Go ahead,' Amanda said to the two youngsters. 'Remember, word of Cletus, or any word of what's going on in town, are the two things I particularly want to hear about.'

There was the faintest rustle of grass, and she was alone with Ramon.

A little over an hour later the two team members were back.

'Nothing much of anything going on,' Lexy reported. 'Nothing about Cletus coming. They'd like some news themselves about how long they're going to be here and what they're going to do. All they say about the town is that it's dull – they say what good would it be if they could go in there? There's no place to drink or anything else going on. They did mention an old lady being sick, but they didn't say which one.'

'Berthe Haugsrud's the oldest,' said Ramon's voice, out of the darkness.

Amanda snorted.

'At their age,' she said, 'anyone over thirty's old. All right, we'll meet here again and try it once more, tomorrow night.'

She left them and swung east to the Aras homestead, to see if the district's single physician, Dr. Ekram Bayar, who had been reported there, had heard word of any sick in Foralie Town.

'He's gone over to Foralie,' Tosca Aras' diminutive daughter told her. 'Melissa phoned to say Betta was going into labor. Ekram said he didn't expect any problems, but since he was closer than any of the medicians, he went himself. But he's coming back here. Do you want to phone over there, now?'

Amanda hesitated.

'No,' she said. 'I've been staying off the air so that whatever listening devices they've got down in the troop area can't be sure where I am. I'll wait a bit, here. Then, if he doesn't come soon, you could call for me and find out how things are.'

'You could take a nap,' said Mene.

'No, I've got things to do,' said Amanda.

But she ended up taking the nap. Mene called her awake on the intercom at what turned out to be an hour and a half later and she came in to the Aras sitting room to find Tosca himself up, with his broken leg stretched out stiffly on a couch, and both Mene and Ekram with the old general, having a drink before dinner.

'Amanda!' Mene said. 'It was a false alarm about Betta.'

'Uh!' Amanda found a chair and dropped heavily into it. 'The pains stopped?'

'Before Ekram even got there.'

Amanda looked across at the physician, a sturdy, brown-faced thirty-year-old with a shock of black, straight hair and a bushy black mustache.

'She probably doesn't need me at all,' he said to Amanda. 'I'd guess she'll have one of the easier births on record around here.'

'You don't know that,' said Amanda.

'Of course I don't know,' he said. 'I'm just giving you my opinion.'

It came to her suddenly that Ekram, like herself and everyone else, had been under an emotional strain since the invasion became a reality. She became aware suddenly of Tosca stretching out an arm in her direction.

'Here,' he said. He was handing her a glass.

'What's this? Whisky? Tosca, I can't –'

'You aren't going any place else tonight,' he said. 'Drink it.'

She became conscious that the others all had glasses in their hands.

'And then you can have dinner,' said Tosca.

'All right.' She took the glass and sipped cautiously at it. Tosca had diluted the pure liquor with enough water so that it was the sort of mixture she could drink with some comfort. She looked over the rim of her glass at the physician.

'Ekram,' she said. 'I had some of the team children listening outside the cantonments. They reported the soldiers had been mentioning someone – an old woman, they said – was sick in town . . .'

'Berthe.' He put down his glass on the coffee table before the couch on which he sat, his face a little grim. 'I should go down there.'

'No,' said Tosca.

'If you get in there, they may not let you out again,' said Amanda. 'They'll have military medicians.'

'Yes. A full physician, a lieutenant colonel – there for the benefit of this Dow deCastries more than for the troops, I'd guess,' Ekram said. 'I've talked to him over the air. Something of a political appointee, I gather. Primarily a surgeon, but he seemed capable, and he said he'd take care of anyone in town when I wasn't there. He expects me to be available most of the time, of course.'

'You told him you had your hands full up here?'

'Oh, yes,' Ekram gnawed a corner of his moustache, something he almost never did. 'I explained that with most of the mothers of young children being upcountry right now. . . .'

He trailed off.

'He accepted that, all right?'

'Accepted it? Of course, he accepted it. I hope you realize, Amanda –' he stared hard at her, 'it's not my job to ignore people.'

'Who're you ignoring? Berthe? You told the truth. You've got patients needing you all over the place, up here.'

'Yes,' he said.

But his gaze was stony. It went off from her to the unlit,

wide stone fireplace across the room and he drank sparsely from his glass, in silence.

'I'll have dinner in a few minutes,' said Mene, leaving them.

With dinner, Ekram became more cheerful. But by the following morning the phone began to ring with calls from other households relaying word they had heard in conversations with people still in the town, of now two or three of the older people there being ill.

'Not one of the ones who're supposed to be sick has called,' Mene pointed out over the breakfast table.

'They wouldn't, of course. Noble – yes, damned noble, all of them! All of you. I'm sorry, Amanda –' he turned stiffly to Amanda. 'I'm going down.'

'All right,' said Amanda.

She had meant to leave early; but she had stayed around, fearing just such a decision from Ekram. They would have to give, somewhat. But they need not give everything.

'All right,' she said again. 'But not until this evening. Not until things are shut down for the day.'

'No,' said Ekram. 'I'm going now.'

'Ekram,' said Amanda. 'Your duty's to everyone. Not just to those in the town. The real need for you may be yet to come. You're our only physician; and we may get to the equivalent of a field hospital before this is over.'

'She's right,' said Tosca.

'Damn it!' said Ekram. He got up from the table, slammed his chair back into place and walked out of the kitchen. 'Damn this whole business!'

'It's hard for him, of course,' said Tosca. 'But you needn't worry, Amanda.'

'All right,' Amanda said. 'Then I'll get going.'

She spent the day out tracking the patrols. In one or two instances, where the sweep was the third through a particular area, the majority at least of the soldiers in a particular patrol were those who had been out on the first sweep – not only to her eyes but the sharper observation of the team members who had been keeping track of those patrols. She watched them closely through a scope, trying to see if there were any signs of sloppiness or inattention evident in the way they performed their duties; but she was unable to convince herself that she saw any.

She had a good deal more success, with the help of the team members, in identifying patterns of behavior that were developing in the way they made their sweeps. Their approach to a household, for one thing, had already begun to settle down to a routine. That was the best clue that the line soldiers had yet given as to their opinion of the dangerousness of those still left in Foralie district. She found herself wondering, briefly, how all the other districts in all the other cantons of the Dorsai were doing with their defense plans and their particular invaders. Some would have more success against the Earth troops, some less – that was inherent in the situation and the nature of things.

She sent word to the households themselves, to the effect that the people in them should, whenever possible, do and say the same thing each time to the patrols so as to build a tendency in these contacts toward custom and predictability.

It was mid-afternoon when a runner caught up with her with a message that had been passed by phone from homestead to homestead for her, in the guise of neighborly gossip.

'Ekram's left the upcountry for town,' she was told. The runner, a fourteen-year-old boy, looked at her with the steady blue eyes of the D'Aurois family.

'Why?' Amanda asked. 'Did whoever passed the message say why?'

'He was at the Kiempii homestead, and he got a call from the military doctor,' the boy said. 'The other doctor's worried about identifying whatever's making people sick in town.'

'That's all?'

'That's all Reiko Kiempii passed on, Amanda.'

'Thank you,' she said.

'– Except that she said the latest word is nothing's happened yet with Betta.'

'Thanks,' Amanda said.

She was a good hour of skimmer time from the Kiempii homestead, it was not far out of her way on her route to meet Lexy, Tim and Ramon once more above the meadow with the cantonment huts. She left her checking on the patrols and headed out.

When she got there, Reiko was outside, waiting, having heard Amanda was on the way. Amanda slid the skimmer to a stop and spoke eye to eye with the calm, tall, bronzed young woman, without getting out of the vehicle.

'The call went to Foralie first,' Reiko told her, 'but Ekram had already moved on. It finally caught up with him here, about two hours ago.'

'Then you don't know what the military doctor told him?'

'No, all Ekram said was that he had to go down, that he couldn't leave it all to the other physician any longer.'

Amanda looked at Maru Kiempii's daughter, bleakly.

'Three hours until dark,' she said, 'before I can get Lexy down to listen to what they're talking about in the cantonments.'

'Eat something. Rest,' said Reiko.

'I suppose so.'

Amanda had never had less appetite or felt less like resting in her life. She could feel events building inexorably toward an explosion, as she had felt the long rollers of the Atlantic surf on the harsh seashores of her childhood, building to the one great wave that would drive spray clear to the high rocks on which she stood watching.

But it was common sense to eat and rest, with much of a long day behind her and possibly a long night ahead.

Just before sunset, she left the Kiempii homestead, and arrived at the meeting place with Lexy, Tim and Ramon before full dark. The clouds were thick and the air that wrapped about them was heavy with the dampness of the impending weather.

'Ekram still in town?' she asked.

'Yes,' said Ramon. 'We've got a cordon circling the whole area, outside the picket line the troops set up around the town. No one's gone out all day but patrols. If Ekram does, we'll get word as soon as he leaves.'

'Good,' said Amanda. 'Lexy, Tim, be especially careful. A night like this their sentries could be in a mood to shoot first and check afterward. And the same thing applies to the soldiers in the cantonment area, itself.'

'All right,' said Lexy.

They went off. Amanda did not offer to talk and Ramon did not intrude questions upon her. Now that she was at the scene of some actual action, she began to feel the fatigue of the day in spite of her rest up at Kiempii homestead, and she dozed lightly, sitting on her skimmer.

She roused at a touch on her arm.

'They're coming back,' said Ramon's voice in her ear.

She sat up creakily and tried to blink the heavy obscurity out of her eyes. But it was almost solid around her. The only thing visible was the line of the ridge-crest, some thirty meters off, silhouetted against the lighter dark of the clouded sky. The clouds were low enough to reflect a faint glow from the lights of the town and the cantonment beyond the ridge.

'Amanda, we heard about Cletus –' It was Lexy's voice, right at her feet. She could see nothing of either youngster.

'What did you hear?'

'Well, not about Cletus, himself, exactly –' put in Tim.

'Practically, it was,' said Lexy. 'They've got word from one of their transport ships, in orbit. It picked up the signal of a ship phasing in, just outside our star system. They think it's Cletus, coming. If it is, they figure that in a couple more short phase shifts he ought to be in orbit here; and he ought to be down on the ground at Foralie by early afternoon tomorrow, at the latest.'

'Did they say anything about their transport trying to arrest him in orbit?'

'No,' said Lexy.

'Did you expect them to, Amanda?' Ramon asked.

'No,' said Amanda. 'He's coming of his own choice and it makes sense to let anything you want all the way into a trap before you close it. Once in orbit, his ship wouldn't be able to get away without being destroyed by theirs, anyway. But mainly, they want to be sure to get him alive for that full-dress trial back on Earth, so they can arrange to have the rest of us deported and scattered. So, I wouldn't expect they'll do anything until he's grounded. But there's always orders that get misunderstood, and commanders who jump the gun.'

'Tomorrow afternoon,' said Ramon musingly. 'That's it, then.'

'That's it,' said Amanda, grimly. 'Lexy, what else?'

'Lots of people in town are sick –' Lexy's voice was unaccustomedly hushed, as if it had finally come home to her what this situation was leading to, with people she had known all her life. 'Both docs are working.'

'How about the soldiers? Any of them sick?'

'Yes, lots,' said Lexy. 'Just this evening, a whole long line of them went on sick call.'

Amanda turned in the direction of Ramon's flitter and spoke to the invisible Ancient.

'Ramon,' she said, 'how many hours was Ekram in town in the afternoon?'

'Not more than two.'

'We've got to get him out of there . . .' But her tone of voice betrayed the fact that she was talking to herself, rather than to the other three, and no one answered.

'I want to know the minute he leaves,' Amanda said. 'If he isn't gone by morning . . . I'd better stay here tonight.'

'If you want to move back beyond the next ridge, we can build you a shelter,' Ramon said. 'We can build it up over you and your skimmer and you can tap heat off the skimmer. That way you can be comfortable and maybe get some sleep.'

Amanda nodded, then remembered they could not see her.

'Fine,' she said.

In the shelter, with the back of her driver's seat laid down and the other seat cushions arranged to make a bed, Amanda lay, thinking. Around her, a circle of cut and stripped saplings had been driven into the earth and bent together at their tops to make the frame. This sagged gently over her head under the weight of the leafy branches that interwove the saplings, the whole crowned and made waterproof by the groundsheet from the boot of the skimmer. In spite of the soft warmth filling the shelter from the skimmer, humming on minimum power to its heater unit, the slight weight of her old down jacket, spread over her shoulders, gave her comfort.

She felt a strange sadness and a loneliness. Present concerns slid off and were lost in personal memories. She found herself thinking once more of Jimmy, her first-born – Betta's grandfather – whom she had loved more than any of her other children, though none of them had known it. Jimmy, whom she had cared for as child and adult through his own long life and all three of her own marriages, and brought at last with her here to the Dorsai to found a household. He was the Morgan from which all the ap Morgans since were named. He had lived sixty-four years, and ended up a good man and a good father – but all those years she had held the reins tight upon him.

Not his fault. As a six-month-old baby he had been taken – legally stolen from her by her in-laws, after his father's death, and the less than a short year and a half of their marriage. She had fought for four years after that, fought literally and legally, until finally she had worn her father- and mother-in-law down to where they were forced to allow her visiting rights; and then she had stolen him back. Stolen him, and fled off-Earth to the technologically-oriented new world of Newton; where she had married again, to give the boy a home and a father.

But when she had finally got him back, he had been damaged. Lying now, in this shelter in the Dorsai hills, she once more faced the fact that it might not have been her

69

in-laws' handling of him that had alone been to blame. It could also have been something genetic in her ancestry and her first husband's. But whatever it was, she had lost a healthy, happy baby, and regained a boy given to sudden near-psychotic outbursts of fury and ill-judgment.

But she had encompassed him, guarded him, controlled him – keeping him always with her and bringing him through the years to a successful life and a quiet death. Only – at a great cost. For she had never been free in all that time to let him know how much she loved him. Her sternness, her unyielding authority, had made up the emotional control he had required, to supply the lack of it in himself. When he lay dying at last, in the large bedroom at Fal Morgan, she had been torn by the desire to let him know how she had always felt. But a knowledge of the selfishness of that desire had sustained her in silence. To put into plain words the role she had played for him all his life would have taken away what pride he had in the way he had lived, would have underlined the fact that without her he could never have stood alone.

So, she had let him go, playing her part to the last. At the very end he had tried to say something to her. He had almost spoken; and a small corner of her mind clung to the thought that there, in the last moment, he had been about to say that he understood, that he had always understood, that he knew how she loved him.

Now, lying in the darkness of the shelter, Amanda came as close as she ever had in her existence to crying out against whatever ruled the universe. Why had life always called upon her to be its disciplinarian, its executioner, as it was doing now, once again? Cheek pressed against the tough, smooth-worn leather of the skimmer seat cushion, she heard the answer in her own mind – it had been because she would do the job and others would not.

She was too old for tears. She drifted off into sleep without feeling the tide that took her out, dry-eyed.

A rustle, the sound of the branches that completely enclosed her being pulled apart, brought her instantly awake. Gray daylight was leaking through the cover below the cap of the groundsheet, and there was the sound of a gust of rain pattering on the groundsheet itself.

'Amanda –' said Ramon, and crawled into the shelter. There was barely room for him to squat beside her skimmer. His face, under a rain-slick poncho hood, was on a level with hers.

She sat up.

'What time is it?'

'Nine hundred hours. It's been daylight for nearly three hours. Ekram's still in town. I thought you'd want to be wakened.'

'Thanks.'

'General Amorine – that brigadier in charge of the troops – has been phoning around the homesteads. He wants you to come in and talk to him.'

'He can do without. Twelve hours,' said Amanda. 'How could I sleep twelve hours? Are the patrols out? How did the troops on them look?'

'A little sloppy in execution. Everybody hunched up – under rain gear of course. But they didn't look too happy, even aside from that. Some were coughing, the team members said.'

'Any news from the homesteads – any news they've heard over the air, by phone from town?'

'Ekram and the military doc were up all night.'

'We've got to get him out of there –' Amanda checked and corrected herself. 'I've got to get him out of there. What's the weather for the rest of today?'

'Should clear by noon. Then cold, windy and bright.'

'By the time Cletus is here we should have good visibility?'

'We should, Amanda.'

'Good. Pass the word. I want those patrols observed all the time. Let me know if you can how many of the men on them become unusually sick or fall out. Also check with Dow's escort troops, at Foralie. Chances are they're all in good shape, but it won't hurt to check. The minute Cletus arrives, pass the word for the four other teams closest to Foralie to move in and join up with your team. Ring Foralie completely with the teams – what's that?'

Ramon had just put a thermos jug and a small metal box on the deck of her skimmer.

'Tea and some food,' Ramon said. 'Mene sent it down.'

'I'm not an invalid.'

'No, Amanda,' said Ramon, backing out through the opening in the shelter on hands and knees. Outside, he pushed the branches back into place to seal the gap he had made entering. Left to herself, her mind busy, Amanda drank the hot tea and ate the equally hot stew and biscuits she found in the metal box.

Finished, she got up and donned her own poncho, dismantled the shelter and put the ground cloth back in the boot, the seat-back and cushions back in place. Outside, the wind was gusty and cold with occasional rain. She lifted her skimmer and slid it down to just behind the lower ridge, where the ponchoed figure of Ramon sat keeping a scope trained on the cantonments and town below.

'I've changed my mind about that commanding officer,' Amanda told him. 'I'm going in to talk to him –'

A gust of wind and rain made her duck her head.

'Amanda?' Ramon was frowning up at her. 'What if he won't let you out again?'

'He'll let me out,' Amanda said. 'But whether I'm there or not, the teams are going to have to be ready to move against deCastries' escort and any troops they send up with Cletus, once Cletus gets to Foralie. Just as they want Cletus for trial, we want Cletus safe, and we want deCastries, alive – not dead. If most of the rest of the districts can't break loose, we want something to bargain with. Cletus'll know how to use deCastries that way.'

'If you're not available and it's time to attack them should we wait for Eachan to come out and take over?'

'If you think there's time – you and the other Ancients. If time looks tight, don't hesitate. Move on your own.'

Ramon nodded.

'I'll look for you here when I come back,' Amanda said; and lifted her skimmer, sending it off at a slant behind the cover of the ridge to approach the town from the opposite, down-river side.

She paused behind a ridge to drop off her handgun and then came up along the river road, where she encountered a Coalition-Alliance sentry in rain gear, about five hundred meters out behind the manufactory. She slid the skimmer directly at him and set it down, half a dozen meters from him. He held his cone rifle pointed toward her as he walked forward.

'Take that gun out of its scabbard, ma'm,' he said, nodding at the pellet shotgun, 'and hand it to me – butt first.'

She obeyed.

He cradled the cone rifle in one arm to take the heavy weight of the pellet gun in both hands. He glanced at it, held it up to look into the barrel and handed it back to her.

'Not much of a weapon, ma'm.'

'No?' Amanda, holding the recovered pellet gun in the crook of her arm, swung it around horizontally until its muzzle rested against the deckface between her and the boot, the deckface over the power unit. 'What if I decide to pull the trigger right now?'

She saw his face go still, caught between shock and disbelief.

'You hadn't thought of that?' said Amanda. 'The pellets from this weapon could add enough kinetic energy to the power core to blow it, you, and me to bits. In your motor pool I could set off a chain explosion that would wipe out your full complement of vehicles. Had you thought of that?'

He stared at her for a second longer, then his face moved.

'Maybe you think you better impound it, after all?'

'No,' he said. 'I don't think you're about to commit suicide, even if they'd let you anywhere near our motor pool – which they wouldn't.'

He coughed.

'What's your business in town, ma'm?'

'I'm Amanda Morgan, mayor of Foralie Town,' she said. 'That's my business. And for that matter, your commanding officer's been asking to see me. Don't tell me they didn't give you an image and a description of me?'

'Yes,' he said. He coughed, lowered his rifle, and wiped from his cheek some of the moisture that had just dripped from the edge of his rain hood. He had a narrow young face. 'You're to go right on in.'

'Then why all this nonsense?'

He sighed a little.

'Orders, ma'm.'

'Orders!' She peered at him. 'You don't look too well.'

He shook his head.

'Nothing important, ma'm. Go ahead.'

She lifted her skimmer and went past him. The sound of the manufactory grew on her ear. She checked the skimmer outside its sliding door, strongly tempted to look inside and see if Jhanis Bins was still at the control board. The town dump looked even less attractive than it ordinarily did. The nickel grindings, which Jhanis had dumped just the other day, had slumped into pockets and hollows; and now these were partially filled with liquid that in the gray day looked to have a yellowish tinge. She changed her mind about going in to look for Jhanis. Time was too tight. She touched the power control bar of the skimmer and headed on into town, feeling the wet, rain-studded wind on the back of her neck.

The streets were empty. Down a side alley she saw a skimmer that she recognized as Ekram's, behind the house of Marie Dureaux. She went on, past the city hall and up to the edge of the cantonment area, where she was again stopped, this time by two sentries.

'Your general wanted to see me,' she said, after identifying herself.

'If you'll wait a moment while we call in, ma'm . . .'

A moment later she was waved through, and directed to a command building four times the size of the ordinary

74

cantonment huts but made of the same blown bubble plastic. Once again she was checked by sentries and ushered, eventually, into an office with a desk, a chair behind it, and one less-comfortable chair facing it.

'If you'll have a seat here,' said the sergeant who brought her in.

She sat and waited for some ten or twelve minutes. At the end of that time a major came in, carrying a folder of record films, which he slipped into the desk viewer, punching up the first one.

'Amanda Morgan?' he said, looking over the top of the viewer, which was slanted toward him, hiding the film on display from her.

'That's right,' said Amanda. 'And you're Major –'

He hesitated.

'Major Suel,' he said, after a second. 'Now, about the situation here in town and in the district –'

'Just a second, Major,' said Amanda. 'I came in to talk to your general.'

'He's busy. You can talk to me. Now, about the situation –'

He broke off. Amanda was already on her feet.

'You can tell the general for me, I don't have time to waste. Next time he can come and find me.' Amanda turned toward the door.

'Just a minute –' There was the sound of the major's chair being pushed back. 'Just a minute!'

'No minute,' said Amanda. 'I was asked to come in to talk to General Amorine. If he's not available, I've got my hands too full to wait around.'

She reached for the door. It did not open for her.

'Major,' she said, looking back over her shoulder. 'Open this door.'

'Come back and sit down,' he said, standing behind his desk. 'You can leave after we've talked. This is a military base –'

He broke off again. Amanda had come back to the desk and walked around it to face the desk viewer. She reached out to press his phone button and the document on the viewer vanished to show the face of the sergeant who had let her in.

'Sir –' the sergeant broke off in confusion, seeing Amanda.

'Sergeant,' said Amanda, 'connect me with Dow deCastries up at Foralie Homestead, right away.'

'Cancel that!' said the major. 'Sergeant – cancel that.'

He punched off the phone and walked to the door.

'Wait!' he threw back at Amanda and went out.

Amanda followed him to the door, but found it once more locked to her touch. She went back and sat down. Less than five minutes later, the major returned with the skin taut over the bones of his face. He avoided looking directly at her.

'This way, if you will,' he said, holding the door open.

'Thank you, Major.'

He brought her to a much larger and more comfortable office, with a tall window against which the rain was now gusting. There was a desk in the corner, but the rest of the furniture consisted of padded armchairs, with the single exception of a single armless straight-backed chair facing the desk. It was to this chair that Amanda was taken.

General Amorine, who had been standing by the window, walked over to seat himself behind the desk.

'I've been trying to get you for two days,' he said.

Amanda, who had not been invited to sit, did so anyway.

'And I've been busy doing what I promised Dow deCastries I'd do,' she said. 'I still am busy at it; and this trip in to see you is delaying it.'

He looked at her, stiff-faced. A cough took him by the throat.

'Mayor,' he said, when the coughing was done, 'you're in no position to push.'

'General, I'm not pushing. You are.'

'I'm the commanding officer of the occupying force here,' he said. 'It's my job to push when things don't work.'

76

He checked, as if he would cough again, but did not. A gust of rain rattled loudly against the office window in the brief moment of silence between them. Amanda waited.

'I said,' he repeated, 'it's my job to push when things don't work.'

'I heard you,' said Amanda.

'They aren't working now,' Amorine said. 'They aren't working to my satisfaction. We want a census of this district and all pertinent data – and we want it without delay.'

'There hasn't been any delay.'

'I think there has.'

Amanda sat, looking at him.

'I know there has,' Amorine said.

'For example?'

He looked at her for several seconds without saying anything.

'How long,' he said, 'has it been since you were on Earth?'

'Seventy years, or so,' said Amanda.

'I thought so,' he said. 'I thought it had been something like that long. Out here on the new worlds, you've forgotten just what Earth is like. Here, on wild planets with lots of space and only handfuls of people even in your largest population centers, you tend to forget.'

'The mess and the overcrowding?'

'The people and the power!' he said, harshly – and broke off to cough again. He wiped his mouth. 'When you think in terms of people out here, you think in terms of thousands – millions, at the most, when your thinking is planet-wide. But on Earth those same figures are billions. You think in terms of a few hundred thousand square meters of floor space given over to manufactory on a whole world. On Earth that space is measured in trillions of square meters. You talk about using a few million kilowatt-hours of energy. Do you know how kilowatt-hours of used energy are counted on Earth?'

'So?' said Amanda.

77

'So –' he coughed. 'So, you forget the differences. Out here for seventy years, you forget what Earth really is, in terms of wealth and strength; and you begin to think that you can stand up against her. The greatest power the human race has ever known looms over you like a giant, and you let yourself dream that you can fight that power.'

'Come into our backyard, and we can fight you,' said Amanda. 'You're a long way from your millions and your trillions now, general.'

'No,' said Amorine, and he said it without coughing or heat. 'That's your self-delusion, only. Earth's got the power to wipe clean every other humanly-settled world whenever she wants to. When Earth moves, when she decides to move, you'll vanish. And you people here are indeed going to vanish. I want you to believe that – for your own sake. You'll save yourself and all the people you love a great deal of pain if you can wake yourself up to an understanding of what the facts are.'

He looked at her. She looked back.

'You are all, all of you, already gone,' he said. 'For the moment you've still got your town, and your homes, and your own name, but all those things are going to go. You, yourself, in your old age, are going to be moved to another place, a place you don't know, to die among strangers – all this because you've been foolish enough to forget what Earth is.'

He paused. She still sat, not speaking.

'There's no reprieve, no choice,' he said. 'What I'm telling you is for your own information only. Our politicians haven't announced it yet – but the Dorsai is already a forgotten world; and everyone on it will soon be scattered individually through all the other inhabited planets. For you – for you, only – I've got an offer, that for you, only, will make things easier.'

He waited, but still she gave him no assistance.

'You're being non-cooperative with our occupation, here,' he said. 'I don't care what Mr. deCastries' opinion of you is. I *know*. I know non-cooperation when I run into it.

I'd be a failure in my job if I didn't. Bear in mind, we don't have to have your cooperation, but it'd help. It'd save paperwork, effort, and explanations. So, what I'm offering you is, cooperate and I'll promise this much for you: I'll ensure that whatever few years you have left can be lived here, on your world. You'll have to watch everyone else being shipped off; but you, at least, won't have to end your days among strangers.'

He paused.

'But you'll have to take me up on this, now,' he said, 'or you'll lose the chance, for good. Say yes now, and follow through, or the chance is gone. Well?'

'General,' said Amanda. 'I've listened to you. Now, you listen to me. You're the one who's dreaming. It's not us who are already dead and gone – it's you and your men. You're already defeated. You just don't know it.'

'Mrs. Morgan,' said Amorine, heavily, 'you're a fool. There's no way you can defeat Earth.'

'Yes,' said Amanda, bleakly. Another gust of rain came and rattled against the window, like the tapping of the fingers of dead children. 'Believe me, there is.'

He stood up.

'All right,' he said. 'I tried. We'll do it our own way from now on. You can go.'

Amanda also stood up.

'One thing, however,' she said. 'I want to see Cletus when he lands.'

'Cletus? Cletus Grahame, you mean?' Amorine stared at her. 'What makes you think he's going to land?'

'Don't talk nonsense, General,' Amanda said. 'You know as well as I do, he's due in by early afternoon.'

'Who told you that?'

'Everyone knows it.'

He stared at her.

'Damn!' he said, softly. 'No, you cannot see Grahame – now or in the future.'

'I've got to be able to report to the local people that he's well and agreeable to being in your custody,' Amanda

79

said. 'Or do you want the district to rise in arms spontaneously?'

He stared at her balefully. Staring, he began to cough again. When the fit was over, he nodded.

'He'll be down in a little over an hour. Shall we find you a place to wait?'

'If it's an hour, I'll go into town and get some things done. Will you leave word at the airpad, so I can get past your soldiers?'

He nodded.

'Ask for Lieutenant Estrange,' he said.

She went out.

Back in town she found Ekram's skimmer still parked behind the house of Marie Dureaux. She parked her own skimmer beside his and let herself in the back door, into the kitchen.

Ekram was there, washing his hands at the sink. He looked back over his shoulder at her at the sound of her entrance.

'Marie?' Amanda said.

'Marie's dead.' He turned his head back to the sink.

'And you're still in town here.'

He finished washing and turned to face her, wiping his hands on a dishtowel.

'Berthe Haugsrud's dead,' he said. 'Bhaktabahadur Rais is dead. Fifteen more are dying. Young Marte Haugsrud's sick. There's five dead soldiers in the cantonments, thirty more dying and most of the rest sick.'

'So you leave,' she said.

'Leave? How can I leave? Their medical officer knows something's going on. There's just nothing he can do about it. He'd be an absolute incompetent idiot not to know that something's going on, particularly since they've been getting word from other occupation units – not from many, but even a few's enough – where the same thing's happening. All that's kept them blind this long is the fact it started hitting our people first. If I run, now –'

He broke off. His face was lean with weariness, stubbled with beard.

'You go,' Amanda said. 'That's an order.'

'To hell with orders!'

'Cletus is due to land in an hour. You've had three hours in town here during daylight hours. In three more hours we're going to have open war. Get out of here, get up in those hills and get ready to handle casualties.'

'The kids . . .' he swayed a little on his feet. 'Kids, kids and guns . . .'

'Will you go?'

'Yes.' His voice was dull. He walked stiff-jointedly past her and out the back door. Following him, she saw him climb, still with the awkwardness of exhaustion, on to his skimmer, lift it, and head it out of town.

Amanda went back inside to see whether there was anything she could do for the remains of Marie. But there was nothing. She left and went to the Haugsrud house to see if Marte could be brought to leave town with her, now that Berthe was dead. But the doors were locked and Marte refused to answer, though Amanda could see her through a window, sitting on the living room couch. Amanda tried several ways to force her way in, but time began to grow short. She turned away at last and headed toward the airpad.

She was almost late getting there. By the time she had made contact with Lieutenant Estrange and been allowed on to the airpad itself, a shuttleboat, bearing the inlaid sunburst emblem of the Exotics, had landed; and Cletus was stepping out on to the pad. A line of vehicles and an armed escort were already waiting for him.

He was wearing a sidearm, which was taken from him, then he was led toward the second of the waiting staff cars.

'I've got to speak to him!' said Amanda fiercely to Estrange. 'Weren't you given orders I was to be able to speak to him?'

'Yes. Please – wait a minute. Wait here.'

The lieutenant went forward and spoke to the colonel

in charge of operations. After some little discussion, Estrange came back and got Amanda.

'If you'll come with me?' He brought her to Cletus, who was already seated in the staff car.

'Amanda!' Cletus looked out over the edge of the open window of the staff car. 'Is everyone all right?'

'Fine,' said Amanda. 'I've taken over the post of Mayor from Piers.'

'Good,' said Cletus, urgently. His cheerful, lean face was a little thinner than when she had seen it last, marked a little more deeply by lines of tension. 'I'm glad it's you. Will you tell everyone they must keep calm about all this? I don't want anyone getting excited and trying to do things. These occupying soldiers have behaved themselves, haven't they?'

'Oh, yes,' said Amanda.

'Good. I thought they would. I'll leave matters in your hands, then. They're taking me up to Grahame House – to Foralie, I mean. Apparently Dow deCastries is already there, and I'm sure once I've had a talk with him we can straighten this all out. So all anyone needs to do is just sit tight for a day or two, and everything will be all right. Will you see the district understands that?'

Out of the corners of her eyes, Amanda could see the almost-wondering contempt growing on the faces of the Coalition officers and men within hearing.

'I'll take care of it, Cletus.'

'I know you will. Oh – how's Betta?'

'You'll see her when you get to Foralie,' said Amanda. 'She's due to have her baby any time now.'

'Good. Good. Tell her I saw her brother David just a few days ago, and he's fine. No – wait. I'll tell her myself, since I'll be seeing her first. Talk to you shortly, Amanda.'

'Yes, Cletus,' said Amanda, stepping back from the staff car. The convoy got underway and moved out.

'And that's this military genius of theirs?' she heard one of the enlisted men muttering to another, as she turned away with Estrange.

Five minutes later she was on her way past the cordon of sentries enclosing the town and twelve minutes after that, having stopped only to pick up her handgun, she stood beside Ramon, on his skimmer, looking down from cover on the more slowly-moving convoy as it headed in the direction of Foralie.

'We'll want all the available teams in position around Foralie before they get there,' she said. 'But when they show up, let them through. We'll want them together with Dow's escort before we hit them.'

'Most of the men in that convoy are sick,' said Ramon.

'Yes,' said Amanda, half to herself. 'But the ones who've been up there with Dow all this time are going to be perfectly healthy. And they're front line troops. If we don't get them in the first few minutes, it's going to cost us –'

'Maybe not,' said Ramon. She looked at him.

'What do you mean?'

'I mean, not all of them up at Foralie may be healthy. I haven't had a chance to tell you, but a patrol came up to there early today and stayed for about two hours. They could have switched personnel.'

'Not likely.' Amanda frowned. 'Dow's their prize package. Why would they take the healthy troops they have protecting him; and replace them with cripples, just to get more of their able-bodied down at town?'

'They might have some reason we don't know about.'

Amanda shook her head.

'I don't believe it,' she said. 'In fact, until I hear positively there's been a change of personnel at Foralie, I won't believe it. We'll continue on the assumption that they're all healthy troops there, and the only advantage we've got is surprise. Cletus, bless him, helped us with that, as much as he could. He did everything possible to put their suspicious to sleep, down in town.'

'He did?' Ramon stared at her. 'What did he do?'

Amanda told him what Cletus had said from the staff

car in the hearing of the convoy soldiery.

Ramon's face lengthened.

'But maybe he really means we shouldn't do anything until . . .'

His voice failed at the look on Amanda's face.

'If a rooster came up to you and quacked,' said Amanda, sharply, 'would you ignore everything else about it and decide it'd turned into a drake?'

She looked down her nose at him.

'Even if Cletus actually had taken leave of his senses, that wouldn't alter the situation for the rest of us,' she went on. 'We've still got to move in, rescue him, and take deCastries when he reaches Foralie. It's the one chance we've got. But don't concern yourself. Cletus understands the situation here.'

She nodded at his skimmer.

'You go get the teams into position. I'll meet you at Foralie before they get there.'

'Where will you be?' Ramon's face was a little pale.

'I'll be rounding up any adults capable of using a weapon – except the women with young children – from the near households. We'll need anyone we can get.'

'What about the other patrols?'

'Once we've got deCastries, we shouldn't have much opposition from anyone else who's been in Foralie Town. A good half of them are going to be dead in a week, and the most of the rest won't be able to fight.'

'They may fight even if they're not able.'

'How can they–' she broke off, suddenly seeing the white look in Ramon's eyes. 'What's the matter with you? You ought to know that.'

'I didn't want to know,' he said. 'I didn't listen when they told us.'

'Didn't you?' said Amanda. 'Well, you'd better listen now, then. Carbon monoxide passed over finely divided nickel gives you a liquid – nickel carbonyl, a volatile liquid that melts at twenty-five degrees Centigrade, boils at forty-three degrees and evaporates at normal temperatures in the open. One part in a million of the vapors can be enough to cause allergic dermatitis and edema of the lungs – irreversible.'

His face was stark. His mouth was open as if he gasped for breath.

'I don't mind the fighting,' he said thickly. 'It's just the thought of the casualties among the soldiers. If this war could only be stopped now, before it starts –'

'Casualties? Before it starts?' Amanda held him with her eyes. 'What do you think Berthe Haugsrud and Bhak and the others have been, down in town?'

He did not answer.

'They're our casualties,' she said, 'already counted. The war you want to stop before it starts has been going for two days. Did you think it would all take place with no cost at all?'

'No, I . . .' He swayed a little on his skimmer; and the momentary gust of anger he had sparked off in her went away, suddenly.

'I know,' she said. 'There're things that aren't easy for you to think about. They aren't easy for Ekram. Nor for me, nor any of us. Nor was it easy for those people like Berthe, down in town, who stayed there knowing what was going to happen to them. But do you have any more of it to face or live with than they did, or the boys and girls on the teams will?'

'No,' he said. 'But I can't help how I feel.'

'No,' she said. 'No, of course you can't. Well, do the best you can, anyway.'

He nodded numbly and reached for the power bar of his skimmer. Amanda watched him lift and slide away, gazing for a long moment after his powerful shoulders, now slumped and weary. Then she mounted her own skimmer and took off at right angles to his route.

She reproached herself as she went, for her outburst at him. He was still young and had not seen what people could do to people. He had no basis of experience from which to imagine what would happen to the dispossessed Dorsai, once they were scattered thinly among the populations of other worlds who had been educated to hold them in detestation and contempt. He could still cling to a hope that somehow an enemy could be defeated with such cleverness that neither friend nor foe need suffer.

She headed toward the Aras homestead to pick up Mene as the first of her adult recruits for the assault on Foralie.

Travelling there, even now, she found the mountains calming her spirit. The rain had stopped, according to the weather predictions Ramon had given her, and a swift wind was tearing the cloud cover to tatters. The sky revealed was a high, hard blue; and the air, on the wings of a stiff breeze, piping with an invigorating cold. She felt stilled, concentrated and clear of mind.

For better or for worse, they must now move into literal combat. There was no more time to worry whether individuals would measure up. There was no time for her cataloguing of the sort of lacks she had noted in Betta, in Melissa, in Lexy and just now in Ramon. Time had run out on her decision of the name for Betta's child. She must leave word with others before the actual assault on Foralie about what she had decided, one way or another, so that it could be passed on to Betta if necessary. She would do just that. At the last minute she would make up her mind one way or another and have done with it.

Forty-five minutes later, she swung her skimmer up to a fold in the hills, carrying Mene Aras with her. As she topped the rise and dipped down into the hidden hollow beyond, she saw the Ancients of five teams; together with a dozen or so of the team-leaders and runners from them, plus Jer Walker leaning on both his walking canes and a half-rifle slung from the shoulders of his frail, ninety-year-old body. Nine of the other women, most of them young, and also armed, were already there. But most welcome of all was the sight of the unusual pair that were Arvid Johnson and Bill Athyer, together with six of the Dorsai they had been able to keep as staff.

Amanda slid her skimmer to a stop, stepped off and walked up to Arvid and Bill.

'I was deliberately not counting on you,' she said, 'but I thought you might be here in time.'

'You'll need us,' Arvid said. 'I take it you knew Swahili is now the officer in charge of Dow's escort? He came up here with replacement troops this morning.'

'Swahili?' Amanda frowned, for the name had a familiar ring but eluded identification.

'He's a major with these Coalition troops. But he was one of Eachan Khan's officers,' Bill said. 'A Dorsai, once – but probably you've never seen him. He didn't like any place where there wasn't any fighting going on. He joined Eachan some years ago, out on one of the off-world contracts and I think he was only here in this district briefly, once or twice. The only things that usually brought him to the Dorsai were short visits to that new training center Cletus set up on the other side of the world.'

'The point is, though, he literally is a Dorsai – or was. One of the best we ever had, in fact,' said Arvid. 'If anyone's going to catch us moving in before we want them to know we're there, it'll be him.'

There was a strange, almost sad note in Arvid's voice.

'Yes, he's that good. Some of us – ' Bill glanced for a second at his tall companion, 'thought he was the best we had . . . in some ways. At any rate, that's why Arvid and I'll be going in first, to secure the house.'

'You're taking charge, then?' said Amanda.

'We hadn't planned on it,' said Arvid, swiftly. 'It's your district, of course –'

'Don't talk nonsense,' said Amanda. 'We'll do anything that works. Did you really think I'd be prickly about my authority?'

'No,' said Arvid. 'Not really. But I do think you should stay in overall command. These local people know you, not me. Just give us four minutes' head start, then move in. We'll take the house. That'll leave you the compound area that was set up for the escort troops, beside the house. How do you plan to handle that?'

'The only way we can,' said Amanda. 'I'll go in first, with the other adults behind me – openly, like neighbors coming to visit – and I'll try to disarm the sentry. Then we'll take the compound – we adults – building by building. Meanwhile, the teams will lie out around with their weapons and try to see that, whatever happens, none of the soldiers break out of the compound area after we've gone in.'

Arvid nodded.

'All right,' he said. 'Our word is that all the men in the convoy bringing Cletus in are pretty well sick and useless. I suppose you also have the information that most of the well troops that came up originally with Dow were traded back to town for the personnel of the patrol that came up with Swahili – a patrol of sick that were sent up this morning? That should make things easier for you.'

Amanda scowled.

'I heard that from Ramon – one of my team Ancients,' she said. 'I don't believe it. Why trade good fighting men for bad around someone as important as Dow?'

'It checks out, all the same,' said Arvid. 'We hear Dow was called by their military physician late last night. He was the one who ordered the change.'

'You monitored that call?'

'No. Just got a report on it, passed out through Foralie town.'

Amanda shook her head stubbornly.

'One further piece of evidence,' said Arvid. 'On the basis of the report, I had a couple of my staff check the patrol that went out and the patrol that came back. It was a completely different set of faces that returned.'

Amanda sighed.

'All right. If that's right . . .' she swung away from him. 'Take off any time you're ready.'

'We're ready now,' said Arvid. 'Four minutes.'

'Good luck,' she said, and went over to her own group, the assorted gang of women, Jer, the five Ancients and the

88

young team-members, carrying their cone and energy rifles in the crook of their arms, muzzle down, like hunting weapons.

'All right,' she said to them all. 'You know what you're supposed to do and you heard me talking just now with Arvid and Bill . . .'

She hesitated, finding herself strangely, uncharacteristically, at a loss for words. There was something that needed to be said; something that she had been working toward for a very long time, that she needed to tell them before they went where they were going. But whatever it was, it would not define itself for her. A skimmer topped the ridge opposite the one that overlooked Foralie and came sliding down to them under full power, carrying Reiko Kiempii, armed. Amanda saw the tall young woman's eyes slip past her for a second to Arvid. Then Reiko had reached the rest of them and jumped off her skimmer.

'I got word over the phone just before I left home,' she said to Amanda. 'Betta's in labor – the real thing, this time.'

'Thanks,' said Amanda, hardly knowing she spoke.

Suddenly, as if a switch had been pulled, the words she had been looking for were ready to her tongue. With this news everything abruptly fell into order – her silent lifelong love for Jimmy and for Fal Morgan, the years of struggling to survive back when the outlaw mercenaries had prowled the new Dorsai settlements, the sending out of the men in each generation to be killed, to earn the necessary credits that alone would let them all continue to survive – just as they were, and wished to be.

As they were.

Those were the magic words. They had a right to be as they were; and it was a right worth all it cost. This harsh world had been one that no one else had wanted. But they had taken it, she and others like her. They had built it with their own hands and blood. It was theirs. *You love*, she thought suddenly, *what you give to – and in proportion as you give.*

That was all she had wanted to say. But now, looking around her at the adolescent faces of the young team members, at the other adult women, at old Jer Walker, she realized there had never been any need to tell the rest of them that. From the youngest to the oldest, they already knew it. It was in their bones and blood, as it was in hers. Perhaps not all of them had yet put it into words in their minds, as she had just done in hers – but they knew.

She looked at them. Mixed in among their living figures she thought she saw the presence of ghosts – of Berthe Haugsrud, of Bhaktabahadur Rais, of Jimmy himself and all those from other households who had died for the Dorsai, both here and on other worlds. Like the mountains, these stood up all around them, patiently waiting.

It came to her then like a revelation that none of it mattered – their individual weaknesses, the things that they seemed to lack that she herself either had innately, or time had taught her. She had been guilty of Amandamorphism – thinking only someone exactly like herself could earn even passing marks to qualify for the role she had played here so long. But that idea was nonsense. The fact that no two people were exactly alike had nothing to do with the fact that two people could be equally useful.

There came a time when everyone had to face the leaving of ultimate decisions to others, and to time itself. A time when faith proved to either have been placed, or misplaced, but when it was too late to do anything more about it. It was not up to her to leave Betta a last decision about the use of the Amanda name for Betta's child. Betta herself was the one to decide that, as Amanda had made necessary decisions in her own time, and all generations to come would have to make their own decisions in their time.

'What are you smiling at, Amanda?' said Reiko,

looming beside and over her.

'Nothing,' said Amanda. 'Nothing at all.'

She turned to the rest of them.

'I'll go in first,' she said, 'as soon as Arvid and Bill with their team have had their four minute lead. The rest of you, follow me, coming two to a skimmer, from different directions. We'll use Betta as an excuse for gathering at Foralie, as long as that's conveniently turned up. Actually, the excuse won't matter . . .'

She looked around at their faces.

'Myself, first. Then Mene and Reiko. The rest team up as you wish. Team members, stay close and fire as needed; but don't move in to the compound unless or until you're called in by one of us who've gone ahead. That includes Ancients. Ancients, stay with your teams. In case everything falls apart here, it'll be up to each of you to pull your team off, get it back into the mountains, and keep it alive. Everybody understand?'

They nodded or murmured their understanding.

'All right –' She was interrupted by a flicker of red, a cloth being waved briefly from just behind the crest of the ridge overlooking Foralie. 'All right. Convoy in sight. It'll take it another five minutes or so to reach the house. Everybody up behind the ridge, ready to go.'

Lying with the others, just behind the crest of the ridge, she looked through a screen of grass at the convoy. Even to her eye, its vehicle column seemed to move somewhat sluggishly. Evidently that part of Arvid's information – about the convoy troops all being sick – was correct. She crossed her fingers mentally upon the hope that the rest of what he had told her was also reliable – but with misgivings. Counting the team members, the Dorsai would outnumber the troops of the convoy and those already at Foralie nearly five to one – but children against experienced soldiers made that figure one of mockery. Experienced soldiers against civilians was bad enough.

The convoy was almost to the house. She pushed herself backwards and got to her feet below the crest of the ridge. Looking over, she saw the last of the Dorsai soldiers belonging to Bill and Arvid already disappearing – they would be crawling forward through the tall grass now, to get as close as they could come to the house before making their move. She checked her watch, counting off the minutes. When four were gone, she waved to the other civilians, mounted her skimmer and took it up over the ridge, directly down upon the single sentry standing in front of the compound of bubble plastic structures at the far end of the house. The convoy had pulled out of sight into the compound just moments before she reached him; and his head was still turned, looking after it. She had set the skimmer down before he belatedly turned to the sound of her power unit. His cone rifle swung up hastily, to cover her.

'Stay right there –' he was beginning, when she interrupted him.

'Oh, stop that nonsense! My great-granddaughter's having a baby. Where is she?'

'Where? She . . . oh, the house, of course, ma'm.'

'All right, you go tell her I'll be right there. I've got to speak to whoever's in charge of that convoy –'

'I can't leave my post. I'm sorry, but –'

'What do you mean, you can't leave your post? Don't you recognize me? I'm the mayor of Foralie Town. You must have been shown an image of me as part of your briefing. Now, you get in there –'

'I'm sorry. I really can't –'

'Don't tell me you can't –'

They argued, the sentry forgetting his weapon to the point where its barrel sagged off to one side. A new humming announced another skimmer that slid down upon them with Reiko and Mene Tosca aboard.

'Halt –' said the soldier, swinging his rifle to command these new arrivals.

'Now what're you doing?' said Amanda, exasperatedly. Out of the corner of her eye, she saw Cletus being escorted into the house. The majority of the soldiers of the convoy should now be out of their vehicles and moving inside one or another of the cantonment buildings. There was still no sign of Arvid, Bill and their team.

'Don't you understand that neighbors come calling when there's a birth?' she said sharply, interrupting another argument that was developing between the sentry and Reiko. 'I know these neighbors well. I'll vouch for them . . .'

'In a second, ma'm . . .' The sentry threw over his shoulder at her and turned back to Reiko.

'No second,' said Amanda.

The difference in the tone of her voice brought him around. He froze at the sight of Amanda's heavy handgun pointed at his middle. Ineffective as they were at ordinary rifle distance, the energy handguns were devastating at point-blank range like this. Even if Amanda's aim should be bad – and she held the gun too steadily to suggest bad aim – any pressure on its trigger would mean his being cut almost in two.

'Just keep talking,' said Amanda softly. She held the gun low, so that the sentry's own body shielded any view of it from the compound or the house. 'You and I are just going on with our conversation. Wave these two to the compound as if you were referring them to someone there. There'll be other skimmers coming –'

'Yes . . . two more. On the way now,' Mene's voice almost hissed, close by her ear.

'– and after each one stops here for a moment, you'll wave them to the compound, too. Do you understand?' Amanda said.

'Yes . . .' His eyes were on the steady muzzle of her handgun.

'Good. Mene, Reiko, go ahead. Wait until enough others catch up with you before you make a move, though.'

'Leave it to us,' said Reiko. Their skimmer lifted and hummed toward the compound.

'Just stand relaxed,' Amanda told the sentry. 'Don't move your rifle.'

She sat. The sentry's face showed the pallor of what was perhaps illness, now overlaid with a mute desperation. He did not move. He was not as youthful as some of the other soldiers, but from the relative standpoint of Amanda's years they were all young. Other skimmers came and moved on to the compound, until all the adults had gone by her.

'Stand still,' Amanda said to the sentry.

Off to one side, a movement caught her eye. It was a figure slipping around the corner of the house and entering the door. Then another. Arvid and Bill with their men – at last.

She turned her head slightly to look. Five . . . six figures flickered around the corner of the house and in through the door. Out of the other corner of her eyes she caught movement close to her. Looking back, she saw the sentry bringing up the barrel of his rifle to knock the energy weapon out of her hand. Twenty, even ten years before, she would have been able to move the handgun out of the way in time, but age had slowed her too much.

She felt the shock against her wrist as metal met metal and the energy gun was sent flying. But she was already stooping to the scabbard with the pellet shotgun as the sentry's cone rifle swung back to point at her. The stream of cones whistled over her bent head, then lowered. She felt a single heavy shock in the area of her left shoulder, but then the shotgun had, in its turn, batted the light frame of the cone rifle aside and the sentry was looking into the wide muzzle of the heavier gun.

'Drop it,' said Amanda.

Her own words sounded distant in her own ears. There was a strange feeling all through her. The impact had been high enough so that possibly the single cone that struck her had not made a fatal wound; but shock was swift with missiles from that weapon.

The cone rifle dropped to the ground.

'Now lie down, face down . . .' said Amanda. She was still hearing her voice as if from a long distance away, and the world about her had an unreal quality to it. 'No, out of arm's reach of the rifle . . .'

The sentry obeyed. She touched the power bar of her skimmer, lifted it and lowered it carefully on the lower half of his body. Then she killed the power and got off. Pinned down by the weight upon him, the sentry lay helpless.

'If you call or struggle, you'll get shot,' she told him.

'I won't,' said the sentry.

There was the whistling of cone rifle fire from the direction of the cantonment. She turned in that direction, but there was no one to be seen outside the buildings she faced. The vehicle park was behind them, however, screened by them from her sight.

She bent to pick up the handgun, then thought better of it. The pellet shotgun was operable in spite of the rust in its barrel, and uncertain as she was now, she was probably better off with a weapon having a wide shot pattern. She began to walk unsteadily toward the compound. Every step took an unbelievable effort and her balance was not good, so that she wavered as she went. She reached the first building and opened its door. A supply room – empty. She went on to the next and opened the door, too wobbly to take ordinary precautions in entering. The thick air of a sickroom took her nostrils as she entered. Tina Alchenso, one of the other women, stood with an energy rifle, covering a barracks-like interior in which all the soldiers there seemed sick or dying. The air seemed heavy as well with the scentless odor of resignation and defeat. Those who were able had evidently been ordered out of their beds. They lay face down on the floor in the central aisle, hands stretched out beyond their heads.

'Where's everybody?' Amanda asked.

'They went on to the other buildings,' Tina said.

Amanda let herself out again and went on, trying

doors as she went. She found two more buildings where one of the adults stood guard over ill soldiers. She was almost back to the vehicle parking area, when she saw a huddled figure against the outside wall of a building.

'Reiko!' she said, and knelt clumsily beside the other woman.

'Stop Mene,' Reiko barely whispered. She was bleeding heavily just above the belt of her jumper. 'Mene's out of her head.'

'All right,' said Amanda. 'You lie quiet.'

With an effort, she rose and went on. There was the next building before her. She opened the door and found Mene holding her energy rifle on yet another room of sick and dying soldiers. Mene's face was white and wiped clean of expression. Her eyes stared, fixed, and her finger quivered on the firing button of the weapon. The gaze of all the men in the room were on her face; and there was not even the sound of breathing.

'Mene,' said Amanda, gently. Mene's gaze jerked around to focus on Amanda for a brief moment before returning to the soldiers.

'Mene . . .' said Amanda, softly. 'It's almost over. Don't hurt anyone, now. It's just about over. Just hold them a while longer. That's all, just hold them.'

Mene said nothing.

'Do you hear me?'

Mene nodded jerkily, keeping her eyes on the men before her.

'I'll be back soon,' said Amanda.

She went out. The world was even more unreal about her and she felt as if she was walking on numb legs. But that was unimportant. Something large was wrong with the overall situation.

Something was very wrong. There were only two more huts shielding her from the vehicle park where the convoy had just unloaded. Those two buildings could not possibly hold all the rest of the original escort, plus the troops of the convoy. Nor should just those two huts be holding two or three of her adults. It did not matter what Arvid had told her. Something had gone astray – she could feel it like a cold weight in her chest below the weakness and unreality brought on by her wound.

She tried to think with a dulled mind. She could gamble that Arvid and Bill's team had already subdued the house; and go back there now, without checking further, to get help . . . her mind cleared a little. A move like that would be the height of foolishness. Even if Arvid and Bill had men to spare to come back here with her, going for assistance would waste time when there might be no time to waste.

She took a good grip on her pellet gun, which was becoming an intolerable weight in her hands, and started around the curved wall of one of the huts.

Possibly the sense of unreality that held her was largely to blame – but it seemed to her that there was no warning at all. Suddenly she found herself in the midst of a tight phalanx of vehicles, the front ones already loaded with weaponed and alert-looking soldiers, and the rear ones with other such climbing into them. But, if her appearance among them had seemed sudden to her, it had apparently seemed the same to them.

She was abruptly conscious that all movement around her had ceased. Soldiers were poised, half-in, half-out of their vehicles. Their eyes were on her.

Plainly, her fears had been justified. The apparent replacement of well soldiers by sick ones had been a trap; and these she faced now were about to move in for a counterattack. She felt the last of her energy and will slipping away, took one step forward, and jammed the muzzle of her pellet shotgun against the side panel shielding the power unit in the closest vehicle.

'Get down,' she said to the officers and men facing her.

They stared at her as if she was a ghost arisen out of the ground before them.

'I'll blow every one of you up if I have to – and be glad to,' she said. 'Get out. Lie down, face down, all of you!'

97

For a second more they merely sat frozen, staring. Then understanding seemed to go through them in an invisible wave. They began to move out of their seats.

'Hurry . . .' said Amanda, for her strength was going fast. 'On the ground . . .'

They obeyed. Dreamily, remotely, she saw them climbing from the vehicles and prostrating themselves on the ground.

Now what do I do? Amanda thought. She had only a minute or two of strength left.

The answer came from the back of her head – the only answer. *Press the firing button of the pellet gun, after all, and make sure no one gets away –*

Unexpectedly, there was the sound of running feet behind her. She started to glance back over her shoulder; and found herself caught and upheld. She was surrounded by the field uniforms of four of the Dorsai staff members who had been with Arvid and Bill.

'Easy . . .' said the one holding her – almost carrying her, in fact. 'We've got it. It's all over.'

There succeeded a sort of blur, and then a large space of nothing at all. At last things cleared somewhat – but only somewhat – and she found herself lying under covers, in one of the Foralie bedrooms. Like someone in a high fever, she was conscious of people moving all around her at what seemed like ungracious speed, and talking words she could not quite catch. Her shoulder ached. Small bits and phrases of dialogue came clear from moment to moment.

'. . . *shai Dorsai!*'

What was that? That ridiculous phrase that the children had made up only a few years back, and which was now beginning to be picked up by their elders as a high compliment? It was supposed to mean 'real, *actual* Dorsai'. Nonsense.

It occurred to her, as some minor statistic might, that she was dying; and she was vaguely annoyed with herself for not having realized this earlier. There were things she should think about, if that was the case. If Betta had been in labor before the attack began, she might well have her child by now.

If so, it was important she tell Betta what she had decided just before they moved in on the troops, that the use of the Amanda name was her responsibility now, and the responsibility of succeeding generations . . .

'Well,' said a voice just above her, and she looked up into the face of Ekram. He stank of sweat and anesthetic. 'Coming out of it, are you?'

'How long . . .' it was incredibly hard to speak.

'Oh, about two days,' he answered with abominable cheerfulness.

She thought of her need to tell Betta of her decision.

'Betta . . .' she said. It was becoming a little easier to talk; but the effort was still massive. She had intended to ask specifically for news of Betta and the child.

'Betta's fine. She's got a baby boy, all parts in good working order. Three point seven three kilograms.'

Boy! A shock went through her.

Of course. But why shouldn't the child be a boy? No reason – except that, deluded by her own aging desires, she had fallen into the comfortable thought that it would not be anything but a girl.

A boy. That made the matter of names beside the point entirely.

For a moment, however, she teetered on the edge of self-pity. After all she had known, after all these years, why couldn't it have been a girl – under happier circumstances when she could have lived to know it, and find that it was a child who could safely take up her name?

She hauled herself back to common sense. What was all this foolishness about names, anyway? The Dorsai had won, had kept itself independent. That was her reward, as well as the reward to all of them – not just the sentimental business of passing her name on to a descendant. But she should still tell Betta of her earlier decision, if Ekram would only let them bring the girl to her. It would be just like the physician to decide that her dying might be hurried by such an effort, and refuse to let Betta come. She would have to make sure he understood this was not a decision for him to make. A deathbed wish was sacred and he must understand that was what this was . . .

'Ekram,' she managed to say faintly. 'I'm dying . . .'

'Not unless you want to,' said Ekram.

She stared at him aghast. This was outrageous. This was too much. After all she had been through . . . then the import of his words trickled through the sense of unreality wrapping her.

'Bring Betta here! At once!' she said; and her voice was almost strong.

'Later,' said Ekram.

'Then I'll have to go to her,' she said, grimly.

She was only able to move one of her arms feebly sideways on top of the covers, in token of starting to get up from the bed. But it was enough.

'All right. All right!' said Ekram. 'In just a minute.'

She relaxed, feeling strangely luxurious. It was all right. The name of the game was survival, not how you did it. A boy! Almost she laughed. Well, that sort of thing happened, from time to time. In a few more years it could also happen that this boy could have a sister. It was worth waiting around to see. She would still have to die someday, of course – but in her own good time.

Interlude

The voice of the third Amanda ceased. In the still mountain afternoon there were no other sounds but the hum of some nearby insects. A little breeze sprang up, and was gone again.

With her words still echoing in his mind, Hal thought of the struggle she had been speaking of, that early Dorsai fight to stay free of Dow deCastries; and its likeness to the present fight on all the worlds, to resist the loss of human freedom to the Other Men and Women – those crossbreeds from human splinter cultures such as that on the Dorsai itself. This present fight in which he and the third Amanda were both caught up.

'What happened inside Foralie?' he asked. 'Inside the house, I mean, after Arvid Johnson and Bill Athyer with their men went inside? What happened with Cletus and Dow – or were they just able to take over with no trouble?'

'Something more than no trouble,' she said. 'Swahili was there, remember, and Swahili had been a Dorsai. But Eachan Khan killed Swahili when Swahili let himself be distracted for a second and Arvid and Bill were able to control the situation. Dow had a sleeve gun of his own, it turned out. He hurt Cletus, but didn't manage to kill him. In the end it was Dow who was shipped back to Earth as a prisoner.'

'I see,' said Hal. But his first question had immediately raised another one in his mind.

'How was that other business worked?' he asked. 'That Coalition trick of having a contingent of well soldiers up there at Foralie after they'd seemed to have been rotated

103

down into the area of town? Where did they come from, the soldiers Amanda found waiting, and ready to fight, in the vehicle park?'

'You remember the military physician had phoned Dow deCastries the night before,' Hal's Amanda said. 'He was a political appointee himself and he knew General Amorine was another. Besides Amorine was sick himself from the nickel carbonyl vapors. The military physician knew that taking his suspicions to Amorine would simply have meant Amorine arresting Ekram and trying to force some kind of answer out of him – and the military doctor was only too aware of what it would be like for him to face alone a situation where everybody was dying. So, he went directly to Dow, instead.'

'I don't understand what that would have to do with it . . .' Hal frowned.

'Dow had been getting the reports from other areas. A thousand different things were going wrong in a thousand different places with his occupation forces; and, next to Cletus, he had the best mind on the planet.' She paused to look at him. 'Don't underestimate what Dow was.'

'I didn't intend to.'

'What he saw,' Amanda said, 'was that, for all practical purposes, his occupation of the Dorsai had failed. But he could still, with some luck, grab Cletus and take him off-planet as a prisoner – or at the worst, get away himself. This, if he had military control in this one district alone.'

'And he figured out that as soon as Cletus reached Foralie, Foralie would be attacked by the local people in a try to rescue him?'

'Of course.' Amanda shrugged. 'It was obvious – as the first Amanda essentially said, to Ramon, when Ramon wondered if Cletus hadn't really meant what he said at the airpad – that they should do nothing against the soldiers. One way or another the district had to attack, then. So he sent up the patrol that morning with only sick soldiers; and it brought back well soldiers, all right; but those same well soldiers – only now pretending to be sick – went

back up as the troops in the convoy that escorted Cletus to Foralie.'

'Ah,' said Hal, nodding. 'How long did the first Amanda actually live?'

'She lived to be a hundred and eight.'

'And saw a second Amanda?'

Hal's Amanda shook her head.

'No. It was nearly a hundred years before there was a second Amanda,' she said.

Hal smiled.

'Who had the wisdom to name the second one Amanda?'

'No one,' Amanda said. 'She was named Elaine; but by the time she was six years old everyone was already calling her the second Amanda. You might say, she named herself.'

Once more, in the back of his mind, Hal felt an obscure alerting to attention of that part of him which recognized the existence of The Purpose.

'Tell me something about the second Amanda,' he said.

The third Amanda hesitated for a brief moment.

'For one thing,' she said, 'the second Amanda was the one both Kensie and Ian Graeme were in love with.'

'Kensie and Ian?' Hal felt a strange coldness move through him. 'But Kensie never married and Ian . . .'

'That's right,' Amanda said. 'Ian's wife, the mother of his children, was named Leah. But it was the second Amanda who both the twins fell in love with in the first place.'

'How did it happen?'

The third Amanda looked down toward Fal Morgan.

'The second Amanda grew up with Kensie and Ian,' she said. 'How could it be any other way when the two households were practically side by side, here? She grew up with them; and by the time they were nearly grown, if she loved either of them, it was probably Kensie, with that brightness and warmth that was such a natural part of him.'

'She loved Kensie?'

'I said – if she loved either of them . . . then. She was young, they were young. She had had them around all her life. What was there about them to make her suddenly fall seriously in love with either one of them? But then they graduated from the Academy and went off to the wars; and when they came back, it was all different.'

She paused.

'Different? How?' Hal said gently, to get her going again.

She sighed once more.

'It's not easy to describe,' she said. 'It's something that happens often, with the situation we have here on the Dorsai. You grow up, knowing the boys of your district, and those from a lot of others. And when they finally sign contracts and go off-planet, that's all they are, still – just tall boys. But then, perhaps it's a year, or several, before they come home; and when they do you find they're . . . different.'

'You mean, they've become men.'

'Not only men,' she said, 'but men you never thought might come from the boys you knew. Some things you hardly noticed about them have moved forward in them and taken over. Other things you thought were the most important part of what made them, have gone way back in them, or been lost forever. They've grown up in ways you didn't expect. Suddenly, it's as if you never had known them. They can be anybody . . . strangers.'

Her voice had sunk so low that she seemed to be speaking more to herself than him; and her gaze was on nothing.

'You sit and talk with them, after they come home,' she went on, 'and you realize you're talking to someone who's gone away from what was common to both of you and now has something that has nothing to do with you, that you've never known and maybe never will know . . .'

She looked at him. Her eyes were brilliant.

'And then you discover that the same thing that happened to them has happened to you. You were a girl they grew up with when they left; but that girl is gone, gone forever. With you, too, some things have come forward, other things have gone back or been lost forever. Now they sit talking to a woman they don't know, that now they maybe never will know. And so, everything changes.'

'I see,' he said. 'And it changed that much for the second Amanda and for Kensie and Ian?'

'Yes,' she said, soberly. 'They came back, two strangers, and fell in love with a stranger they had once grown up with. With any other three people that would have been problem enough – but those twins were half and half of each other, and Amanda knew it.'

'What happened?'

The third Amanda, Hal's Amanda, did not answer. She had drawn her knees up to her chin, and hugged them. Now she rested her chin upon her knees, staring down into the valley.

'What happened?' Hal asked again.

'Everybody had simply assumed that Kensie and Amanda would end up together,' she said, at last, 'including Ian. When Ian found he was in love with Amanda himself, it was unthinkable to him that he should interfere in any way with his twin brother. So he married Leah, who had wanted him for a long time. Married her simply and quickly.'

'And took himself out of the picture.'

'No,' Amanda shook her head. 'Because he had made a mistake. After the two of them had come home, different, it wasn't Kensie, but Ian, that the second Amanda had fallen in love with. Ian. Only with Ian being the kind of person he was, there was no chance that, having once married Leah, that situation could ever be changed.'

'But you say . . .' began Hal puzzled, then checked himself. 'But, if she had any love for Kensie at all, what was to keep her from ending up with him? Certainly that would have been better than the two of them –'

'The way they were.' Amanda turned her head to look at

107

Hal. 'Kensie and Ian were too close not to know each other's feelings; and Kensie loved Amanda as completely as Amanda loved Ian. Knowing how she loved Ian, Kensie could not take the place he would have filled in her life if things had been otherwise. He went back to the wars as if . . . he was too much a Dorsai to deliberately put himself in the way of getting killed. But for all his brightness, he lived in the shadow of death for years after that; and it seemed as if death was perversely avoiding him.'

She looked away from him, down to the valley again.

'The Exotics say,' she went on, 'that there are ontogenetic laws which explain why someone like Kensie could lead a charmed life under such conditions.'

'Yes,' said Hal. He had not realized how strangely he had said the word until he looked up and saw her gazing at him.

'You know something about ontogenetics?' she asked. 'Something that applies to the second Amanda, and Ian and Kensie?'

'To Ian and Kensie, maybe,' he said. The part of him that concerned itself with what he called The Purpose – that half-seen thing he must do with his life – was working powerfully, now; and he heard his own words almost as if someone else was speaking them. 'Ontogenetics merely says nothing happens by chance or accident. Everything is interrelated. Stop and think. When Donal Graeme was moving toward his goal of bringing all the inhabited worlds under one order, his enemy was William of Ceta, just as Dow deCastries was the special opponent of Cletus Grahame.'

'Yes,' Amanda frowned. 'But what of it?'

'To defeat William, who had unlimited power and wealth, Donal needed to defeat all possible military opponents. To do that he needed a military force larger than had ever been seen on the inhabited worlds. Only one other man could train that force as Donal needed it trained – and the rule in the Graeme household was that no two of their men served in the same place at the same

108

time; for the same reason that a father and mother of young children may travel by different spacecraft, so that in case a phase shift accident should take one of them, the other would still be there to take care of the children.'

'But it was different with Ian and Kensie,' Amanda said. 'They were allowed to serve in the same force, together.'

'Until Kensie's death. Then the rule was broken once more by Eachan Khan Graeme, who you'll remember was the family head, Donal's father and Ian's older brother.' The Purpose-oriented part of Hal's mind was in complete control of him, now. He went on, not noticing the sudden intensity with which she was regarding him. 'He asked Donal to find work with him for Ian, as the only means of rousing Ian after his twin's death.'

She was watching him closely.

'You know a good deal about the Graemes,' she said.

Suddenly aware of her attention, he grew flustered.

'I . . . don't,' he said. 'I only know something about ontogenetics.'

'What you're saying adds up to the fact that Donal had Kensie killed to free Ian for his own use.'

'No, no . . .' he protested. 'Only Donal's need for Ian, acting on the network of cause and effect –'

'No!' she said. 'Do you think any such forces could combine to kill Kensie, and Ian wouldn't be aware of it? They were one person, those twins!'

'But you said yourself that Kensie had been searching for death, ever since he had lost Amanda,' he protested. 'Maybe Ian simply, at last, let him go. You remember Kensie was assassinated. Dorsai aren't easy to assassinate, unless they don't care any more –'

'No!' the third Amanda said, again, almost violently. 'That wasn't the way it was, at all. You don't know . . . did you know that Tomas Velt, the Blauvain chief of police, wrote Eachan Khan Graeme afterwards, telling him the whole story? Velt was there and saw it all. Do you know what he saw?'

'No,' said Hal. The part of him concerned with The

Purpose drew close to the front of his mind and spoke through his lips almost against his will, as if it, not he, controlled them. 'But I want to know.'

'I'll tell you, then,' said Amanda, 'I'll tell it all to you, just as I read it when I was young – just as Velt wrote it to Eachan Khan Graeme after Kensie's body had been shipped home here for burial . . .'

Brothers

Physically, he was big, very big. The professional soldiers of several generations from that small, harsh world called the Dorsai, are normally larger than men from other worlds; but the Graemes are large even among the Dorsai. At the same time, like his twin brother, Ian, Commander Kensie Graeme was so well-proportioned in spite of his size that it was only at moments like this, when I saw him standing next to a fellow Dorsai like his executive officer, Colonel Charley ap Morgan, that I could realize how big he actually was. He had the black, curly hair of the Graemes, the heavy-boned face and brilliant grey-green eyes of his family; also, that utter stillness at rest and that startling swiftness in motion that was characteristic of the several-generations Dorsai.

So, too, had Ian, back in Blauvain; for physically the twins were the image of each other. But otherwise, temperamentally, their difference was striking. Everybody loved Kensie. He was like some golden god of the sunshine. While Ian was dark and solitary as the black ice of a glacier in a land where it was always night.

'. . . Blood,' Pel Sinjin had said to me on our drive out here to the field encampment of the Expedition. 'You know what they say, Tom. Blood and ice water, half-and-half in his veins, is what makes a Dorsai. But something must have gone wrong with those two when their mother was carrying them. Kensie got all the blood. Ian . . .'

He had let the sentence finish itself. Like Kensie's own soldiers, Pel had come to idolize the man, and downgrade Ian in proportion. I had let the matter slide.

Now, Kensie was smiling at us, as if there was some joke

we were not yet in on.

'A welcoming committee?' he said. 'Is that what you are?'

'Not exactly,' I said. 'We came out to talk about letting your men into Blauvain city for rest and relaxation; now that you've got those invading soldiers from the Friendly Worlds all rounded up, disarmed, and ready for shipment home – what's the joke?'

'Just,' said Charley ap Morgan, 'that we were on our way into Blauvain to see you. We just got a repeater message that you and other planetary officials here on St. Marie are giving Ian and Kensie, with their staffs, a surprise victory dinner in Blauvain this evening.'

'Hells Bells!' I said.

'You hadn't been told?' Kensie asked.

'Not a damn word,' I said.

It was typical of the fumbling of the so-called government-of-mayors we had here on our little world of St. Marie. Here was I, Superintendent of Police in Blauvain – our capital city – and here was Pel, commanding general of our planetary militia which had been in the field with the Exotic Expedition sent to rescue us from the invading puritan fanatics from the Friendly Worlds; and no one had bothered to tell either one of us about a dinner for the two Commanders of that Expedition.

'You're going in, then?' Pel asked Kensie. Kensie nodded. 'I've got to call my HQ.'

Pel went out. Kensie laughed.

'Well,' he said, 'this gives us a chance to kill two birds at once. We'll ride back with you and talk on the way. Is there some difficulty about Blauvain absorbing our men on leave?'

'Not that way,' I said. 'But even though the Friendlies have all been rounded up, the Blue Front is still with us in the shape of a good number of political outlaws and terrorists that want to pull down our present government. They lost the gamble they took when they invited in the

114

Friendly troops; but now they may take advantage of any trouble that can be stirred up around your soldiers while they're on their own in the city.'

'There shouldn't be any,' Kensie reached for a dress gun-belt of black leather and began to put it on over the white dress uniform he was already wearing. 'But we can talk about it, if you like. You'd better be doing some dressing yourself, Charley.'

'On my way,' said Charley ap Morgan; and went out.

So, fifteen minutes later, Pel and I found ourselves headed back the way we had come, this time with three passengers. I was still at the controls of the police car as we slid on its air cushion across the rich grass of our St. Marie summer toward Blauvain; but Kensie rode with me in front, making me feel small beside him – and I am considered a large man among our own people on St. Marie. Beside Kensie, I must have looked like a fifteen-year-old boy in relative comparison. Pel was equally small in back between Charley and a Dorsai Senior Commandant named Chu Van Moy – a heavy-bodied, black Mongol, if you can imagine such a man, from the Dorsai South Continent.

'. . . No real problem,' Kensie was saying as we left the grass at last for the vitreous road surface leading us in among the streets and roads of the city – in particular the road curving in between the high office buildings of Blauvain's West Industrial Park, now just half a kilometer ahead, 'we'll turn the men loose in small groups if you say. But there shouldn't be any need to worry. They're mercenaries, and a mercenary knows that civilians pay his wages. He's not going to make any trouble which would give his profession a bad name.'

'I don't worry about your men,' I said. 'It's the Blue Front fabricating some trouble in the vicinity of some of your men and then trying to pin the blame on them, that worries me. The only way to guard against that is to have your troops in small enough numbers so that my police-men can keep an eye on the civilians around them.'

'Fair enough,' said Kensie. He smiled down at me. 'I hope, though, you don't plan on having your men holding our men's hands all through their evenings in town –'

Just then we passed between the first of the tall office buildings. A shadow from the late morning sun fell across the car, and the high walls around us gave Kensie's last words a flat echo. Right on the heels of those words – in fact, mixed with them – came a faint sound as of multiple whistlings about us; and Kensie fell forward, no longer speaking, until his forehead against the front windscreen stopped him from movement.

The next thing I knew I was flying through the air, literally. Charley ap Morgan had left the police car on the right side, dragging me along with a hand like a steel clamp on my arm, until we ended up against the front of the building on our right. We crouched there, Charley with his dress handgun in his fist and looking up at the windows of the building opposite. Across the narrow way, I could see Chu Van Moy with Pel beside him, a dress gun also in Chu's fist. I reached for my own police beltgun, and remembered I was not wearing it.

About us there was utter silence. The narrow little projectiles from one or more silver rifles, that had fluted about us, did not come again. For the first time I realized there was no one on the streets and no movement to be seen behind the windows about us.

'We've got to get him to a hospital,' said Pel, on the other side of the street. His voice was strained and tight. He was staring fixedly at the still figure of Kensie, still slumped against the windscreen.

'A hospital,' he said again. His face was as pale as a sick man's.

Neither Charley nor Chu paid any attention. Silently they were continuing to scan the windows of the building opposite them.

'A hospital!' shouted Pel, suddenly.

Abruptly, Charley got to his feet and slid his weapon back into its holster. Across the street, Chu also was rising. Charley looked at the other Dorsai.

'Yes,' said Charley, 'where is the nearest hospital?'

But Pel was already behind the controls of the police car. The rest of us had to move or be left behind. He swung the car toward Blauvain's Medical Receiving, West, only three minutes away.

He drove the streets like a madman, switching on the warning lights and siren as he went. Screaming, the vehicle careened through traffic and signals alike, to jerk to a stop behind the ambulance entrance at Medical West. Pel jumped from the car.

'I'll get a life support system – a medician –' he said, and ran inside.

I got out; and then Charley and Chu got out, more slowly. The two Dorsais were on opposite sides of the car.

'Find a room,' Charley said. Chu nodded and went after Pel through the ambulance entrance.

Charley turned to the car. Gently, he picked up Kensie in his arms, the way you pick up a sleeping child, gently, holding Kensie to his chest so that Kensie's head fell in to rest on Charley's left shoulder. Carrying his Field Commander, Charley turned and went into the medical establishment. I followed.

Inside, there was a long corridor with hospital personnel milling about. Chu stood by a doorway a few meters down the hall to the left, half a head taller than the people between us. With Kensie in his arms, Charley went toward the other Commandant.

Chu stood aside as Charley came up. The door swung back automatically, and Charley led the way into a room with surgical equipment in sterile cases along both its sides, and an operating table in its center. Charley laid Kensie softly on the table, which was almost too short for his tall body. He put the long legs together, picked up the arms and laid their hands on the upper thighs. There was a line of small, red stains across the front of his jacket, high up, but no other marks. Kensie's face, with its eyes closed, looked blindly to the white ceiling overhead.

'All right,' said Charley. He led the way back out into the hall. Chu came last and turned to click the lock on the door into place, drawing his handgun.

'What's this?' somebody shouted at my elbow, pushing toward Chu. 'That's an emergency room. You can't do that –'

Chu was using his handgun on low aperture to slag the lock of the door. A crude but effective way to make sure that the room would not be opened by anyone with anything short of an industrial, heavy-duty torch. The man who was talking was middle-aged, with a grey mustache and the short green jacket of a senior surgeon. I intercepted him and held him back from Chu.

'Yes, he can,' I said, as he turned to stare furiously in my direction. 'Do you recognize me? I'm Tomas Velt, the Superintendent of Police.'

He hesitated, and then calmed slightly – but only slightly.

'I still say –' he began.

'By the authority of my office,' I said, 'I do now deputize you as a temporary Police Assistant. That puts you under my orders. You'll see that no one in this hospital tries to open that door or get into that room until Police authorization is given. I make you responsible. Do you understand?'

He blinked at me. But before he could say anything, there was a new outburst of sound and action; and Pel broke into our group, literally dragging along another man in a senior surgeon's jacket.

'Here!' Pel was shouting. 'Right in here. Bring the life support –'

He broke off, catching sight of Chu.

'What?' he said. 'What's going on? Is Kensie in there? We don't want the door sealed –'

'Pel,' I said. I put my hand on his shoulder. 'Pel!'

He finally felt and heard me. He turned a furious face in my direction.

'Pel,' I said quietly, but slowly and clearly to him. 'He's

118

dead. Kensie. Kensie is dead.'

Pel stared at me.

'No,' he said irritably, trying to pull away from me. I held him. '*No!*'

'Dead,' I said, looking him squarely in the eyes. 'Dead, Pel.'

His eyes stared back at me, then seemed to lose their focus and stare off at something else. After a little they focused back on mine again and I let go of him.

'Dead?' he repeated. It was hardly more than a whisper.

He walked over and leaned against one of the white-painted corridor walls. A nurse moved toward him and I signalled her to stop.

'Just leave him alone for a moment,' I said. I turned back to the two Dorsai officers who were now testing the door to see if it was truly sealed.

'If you'll come to Police Headquarters,' I said, 'we can get the hunt going for whoever did it.'

Charley looked at me briefly. There was no more friendly humor in his face now; but neither did it show any kind of shock, or fury. The expression it showed was only a businesslike one.

'No,' he said briefly. 'We have to report.'

He went out, followed by Chu, moving so rapidly that I had to run to keep up with their long strides. Outside the door, they climbed back into the police car, Charley taking the controls. I scrambled in behind them and felt someone behind me. It was Pel.

'Pel,' I said. 'You'd better stay –'

'No. Too late,' he said.

And it was too late. Charley already had the police car in motion. He drove no less swiftly than Pel had driven, but without madness. For all that, though, I made most of the trip with my fingers tight on the edge of my seat; for with the faster speed of Dorsai reflexes he went through available spaces and openings in traffic where I would have sworn we could not get through.

We pulled up before the office building attached to the

Exotic Embassy as space for Expeditionary Base Head-quarters. Charley led the way in past a guard, whose routine challenge broke off in mid-sentence as he recognized the two of them.

'We have to talk to the Base Commander,' Charley said to him. 'Where's Commander Graeme?'

'With the Blauvain Mayor, and the Outbond.' The guard, who was no Dorsai, stammered a little. Charley turned on his heel. 'Wait – sir, I mean the Outbond's with *him*, here in the Commander's office.'

Charley turned again.

'We'll go on in. Call ahead,' Charley said.

He led the way, without waiting to watch the guard obey, down a corridor and up an escalator ramp to an outer office where a young Force-Leader stood up behind his desk at the sight of us.

'Sir –' the Force-Leader said to Charley, 'the Outbond and the Mayor will only be with the Commander another few minutes –'

Charley brushed past him, and the Force-Leader spun around to punch at his desk phone. Heels clicking on the polished stone floor, Charley led us toward a further door and opened it, stepping into the office beyond. We followed him there – into a large, square room with windows overlooking the city and our own broad-shouldered Mayor, Moro Spence, standing there with a white-haired, calm-faced, hazel-eyed man in a blue robe, both facing a desk at which sat the mirror image of Kensie that was his twin brother, Ian Graeme.

Ian spoke to his desk as we came in.

'It's all right,' he said. He punched a button and looked up at Charley, who went forward with Chu beside him, to the very edge of the desk, and then both saluted.

'What is it?' asked Ian.

'Kensie,' said Charley. His voice became formal. 'Field Commander Kensie Graeme has just been killed, sir, as we were on our way into the city.'

For perhaps a second – no longer – Ian sat without

speaking. But his face – so like Kensie's and yet so different – did not change expression.

'How?' he asked, then.

'By assassins we couldn't see,' Charley answered. 'Civilians we think. They got away.'

Moro Spence swore.

'The Blue Front!' he said. 'Ian . . . Ian, listen . . .'

No one paid any attention to him. Charley was briefly recounting what had happened from the time the message about the invitation had reached the encampment –

'But there wasn't any celebration like that planned!' protested Moro Spence, to the deaf ears around him. Ian sat quietly, his harsh, powerful face half in shadow from the sunlight coming in the high window behind him, listening as he might have listened to a thousand other reports. There was still no change visible in him; except perhaps that he, who had always been remote from everyone else, seemed even more remote now. His heavy forearms lay on the desktop, and the massive hands that were trained to be deadly weapons in their own right lay open and still on the papers beneath them. Almost, he seemed to be more legendary character than ordinary man; and that impression was not mine alone, because behind me I heard Pel hiss on a breath of sick fury indrawn between his teeth; and I remembered how he had talked of Ian being only ice and water, Kensie only blood.

The white-haired man in the blue robe, who was the Exotic, Padma, Outbond to St. Marie for the period of the Expedition, was also watching Ian steadily. When Charley was through with his account, Padma spoke.

'Ian,' he said; and his calm, light baritone seemed to linger and reecho strangely on the ear, 'I think this is something best handled by the local authorities.'

Ian glanced at him.

'No,' he answered. He looked at Charley. 'Who's Duty Officer?'

'Ng'kok,' said Charley.

Ian punched the phone button on his desk.

'Get me Colonel Waru Ng'kok, Encampment HQ,' he said to the desk.

' "No?" ' echoed Moro. 'I don't understand, Commander. We can handle it. It's the Blue Front, you see. They're an outlawed political –'

I came up behind him and put my hand on his shoulder. He broke off, turning around.

'Oh, Tom!' he said, on a note of relief. 'I didn't see you before. I'm glad you're here –'

I put my finger to my lips. He was politician enough to recognize that there are times to shut up. He shut up now; and we both looked back at Ian.

'. . . Waru? This is Base Commander Ian Graeme,' Ian was saying to his phone. 'Activate our four best Hunter Teams; and take three Forces from your on-duty troops to surround Blauvain. Seal all entrances to the city. No one allowed in or out without our authority. Tell the involved troops briefing on these actions will be forthcoming.'

As professional, free-lance soldiers, under the pattern of the Dorsai contract – which the Exotic employers honored for all their military employees – the mercenaries were entitled to know the aim and purpose of any general orders for military action they were given. By a ninety-six per cent vote among the enlisted men concerned, they could refuse to obey the order. In fact, by a hundred per cent vote, they could force their officers to use them in an action they themselves demanded. But a hundred per cent vote was almost unheard of. The phone grid in Ian's desk top said sor...ething I could not catch.

'No,' replied Ian, 'that's all.'

He clicked off the phone and reached down to open a drawer in his desk. He took out a gunbelt – a working, earth-colored gunbelt unlike the dress one Kensie had put on earlier – with sidearm already in its holster; and, standing up, began to strap it on. On his feet, he dominated the room, towering over us all.

'Tom,' he said, looking at me, 'put your police to work, finding out what they can. Tell them all to be prepared to

122

obey orders given by any one of our soldiers, no matter what his rank.'

'I don't know if I've got the authority to tell them that,' I said.

'I've just given you the authority,' he answered calmly. 'As of this moment, Blauvain is under martial law.'

Moro cleared his throat; but I jerked a hand at him to keep him quiet. There was no one in this room with the power to deal with Ian's authority now, except the gentle-faced man in the blue robe. I looked appealingly at Padma, and he turned from me to Ian.

'Naturally, Ian, measures will have to be taken, for the satisfaction of the soldiers who knew Kensie,' Padma said softly, 'but perhaps finding the guilty men would be better done by the civilian police without military assistance?'

'I'm afraid we can't leave it to them,' said Ian briefly. He turned to the other two Dorsai officers. 'Chu, take command of the Forces I've just ordered to cordon the city. Charley, you'll take over as Acting Field Commander. Have all the officers and men in the encampment held there, and gather back any who are off post. You can use the office next to this one. We'll brief the troops in the encampment, this afternoon. Chu can brief his forces as he posts them around the city.'

The two turned and headed toward the door.

'Just a minute, gentlemen!'

Padma's voice was raised only slightly. But the pair of officers paused and turned for a moment.

'Colonel ap Morgan, Commandant Moy,' said Padma, 'as the official representative of the Exotic Government, which is your employer, I relieve you from the requirement of following any further orders of Commander Ian Graeme.'

Charley and Chu looked past the Exotic, to Ian.

'Go ahead,' said Ian. They went. Ian turned back to Padma. 'Our contracts provide that officers and men are not subject to civilian authority while on active duty, engaged with an enemy.'

123

'But the war – the war with the Friendly invaders – is over,' said Moro.

'One of our soldiers has just been killed,' said Ian. 'Until the identity of the killers is established, I'm going to assume we're still engaged with an enemy.'

He looked again at me.

'Tom,' he said. 'You can contact your Police Headquarters from this desk. As soon as you've done that, report to me in the office next door, where I sent Charley.'

He came around the desk and went out. Padma followed him. I went to the desk and put in a phone call to my own office.

'For God's sake, Tom!' said Moro to me, as I punched phone buttons for the number of my office, and started to get the police machinery rolling. 'What's going on here?'

I was too busy to answer him. Someone else was not.

'He's going to make them pay for killing his brother,' said Pel savagely, from across the room. 'That's what's going on!'

I had nearly forgotten Pel. Moro must have forgotten him absolutely; because he turned around to him now as if Pel had suddenly appeared on the scene in a cloud of fire and brimstone-odorous smoke.

'Pel?' he said. 'Oh, Pel – get your militia together and under arms, right away. This is an emergency –'

'Go to hell!' Pel answered him. 'I'm not going to lift a finger to keep Ian from hunting down those assassins. And no one else in the militia who knew Kensie Graeme is going to lift a finger, either.'

'But this could bring down the government!' Moro was close to the idea of tears, if not to the actual article. 'This could throw St. Marie back into anarchy; and the Blue Front will take over by default!'

'That's what the planet deserves,' said Pel, 'when it lets men like Kensie be shot down like dogs – men who came here to risk their lives to save our government!'

'You're crazier than these mercenaries are!' said Moro, staring at him. Then a touch of hope lifted Moro's drawn

124

features. 'Actually, Ian seems calm enough. Maybe he won't –'

'He'll take this city apart if he has to,' said Pel, savagely. 'Don't blind yourself.'

I had finished my phoning. I punched off, and straightened up, looking at Pel.

'I thought you told me there was nothing but ice and water to Ian?' I said.

'There isn't,' Pel answered. 'But Kensie's his twin brother. That's the one thing he can't sit back from and shuffle off. You'll see.'

'I hope and pray I don't,' I said; and I left the office for the one next door where Ian was waiting for me. Pel and Moro followed; but when we came to the doorway of the other office, there was a soldier there who would let only me through.

'. . . We'll want a guard on that hospital room, and a Force guarding the hospital itself,' Ian was saying slowly and deliberately to Charley ap Morgan as I came in. He was standing over Charley, who was seated at a desk. Back against a wall stood the silent figure in a blue robe that was Padma. Ian turned to face me.

'The troops at the encampment are being paraded in one hour,' he said. 'Charley will be going out to brief them on what's happened. I'd like you to go with him and be on the stand with him during the briefing.'

I looked back at him, up at him. I had not gone along with Pel's ice-and-water assessement of the man. But now for the first time I began to doubt myself and begin to believe Pel. If ever there had been two brothers who had seemed to be opposite halves of a single egg, Kensie and Ian had been those two. But here was Ian with Kensie dead – perhaps the only living person on the eleven human-inhabited worlds among the stars who had loved or understood him – and Ian had so far shown no more emotion at his brother's death than he might have on discovering an incorrect Order of the Day.

It occurred to me then that perhaps he was in emotional

shock – and this was the cause of his unnatural calmness. But the man I looked at now had none of the signs of a person in shock. I found myself wondering if any man's love for his brother could be hidden so deep that not even that brother's violent death could cause a crack in the frozen surface of the one who went on living.

If Ian was repressing emotion that was due to explode sometime soon, then we were all in trouble. My Blauvain police and the planetary militia together were toy soldiers compared to these professionals. Without the Exotic control to govern them, the whole planet was at their mercy. But there was no point in admitting that – even to ourselves – while even the shadow of independence was left to us.

'Commander,' I said. 'General Pel Sinjin's planetary militia were closely involved with your brother's forces. He would like to be at any such briefing. Also, Moro Spence, Blauvain's Mayor and protem President of the St. Marie Planetary Government, would want to be there. Both these men, Commander, have as deep a stake in this situation as your troops.'

Ian looked at me.

'General Sinjin,' he said, after a moment. 'Of course. But we don't need mayors.'

'St. Marie needs them,' I said. 'That's all our St. Marie World Council is, actually – a collection of mayors from our largest cities. Show that Moro and the rest mean nothing, and what little authority they have will be gone in ten minutes. Does St. Marie deserve that from you?'

He could have answered that St. Marie had been the death of his brother – and it deserved anything he wished to give it. But he did not. I would have felt safer with him if he had. Instead, he looked at me as if from a long, long distance for several seconds, then over at Padma.

'You'd favor that?' he asked.

'Yes,' said Padma. Ian looked back at me.

'Both Moro and General Sinjin can go with you, then,' he said. 'Charley will be leaving from here by air in about

126

forty minutes. I'll let you get back to your own responsibilities until then. You'd better appoint someone as liaison from your police, to stand by here in this office.'

'Thanks,' I said. 'I will.'

I turned and went out. As I left, I heard Ian behind me, dictating.

'. . . All travel by the inhabitants of the City of Blauvain will be restricted to that which is absolutely essential. Military passes must be obtained for such travel. Inhabitants are to stay off the streets. Anyone involved in any gathering will be subject to investigation and arrest. The City of Blauvain is to recognize the fact that it is now under martial, not civil, law . . .'

The door closed behind me. I saw Pel and Moro waiting in the corridor.

'It's all right,' I told them, ' you haven't been shut out of things – yet.'

We took off from the top of that building, forty minutes later, Charley and myself up in the control seats of a military eight-man liaison craft with Pel and Moro sitting back among the passenger seats.

'Charley,' I asked him, in the privacy of our isolation together up front in the craft, once we were airborne. 'What's going to happen?'

He was looking ahead through the forward vision screen and he did not answer for a moment. When he did, it was without turning his head.

'Kensie and I,' he said softly, almost absently, 'grew up together. Most of our lives we've been in the same place, working for the same employers.'

I had thought I knew Charley ap Morgan. In his cheerfulness, he had seemed more human, less of a half-god of war than other Dorsai like Kensie or Ian – or even lesser Dorsai officers like Chu. But now he had moved off with the rest. His words took him out of my reach, into some cold, high, distant country where only Dorsai lived. It was a land I could not enter, the rules of which I would never understand. But I tried again, anyway.

'Charley,' I said, after a moment of silence, 'that doesn't answer what I asked you.'

He looked at me then, briefly.

'I don't know what's going to happen,' he said.

He turned his attention back to the controls. We flew the rest of the way to the encampment without talking. When we landed, we found the entire Expedition drawn up in formation. They were grouped by Forces into Battalion and Arm Groups; and their dun-colored battle dress showed glints of light in the late afternoon sunlight. It was not until we mounted the stand facing them that I recognized the glitter for what it was. They had come to the formation under arms, all of them – although that had not been in Ian's orders. Word of Kensie had preceded us. I looked at Charlie; but he was paying no attention to the weapons.

The sun struck at us from the southwest at a lowered angle. The troops were in formation, with their backs to the old factory, and when Charley spoke, the amplifiers caught up his voice and carried it out over their heads.

'Troops of the Exotic Expeditionary Force in relief of Saint Marie,' he said. 'By order of Commander Ian Graeme, this briefing is ordered for the hundred and eighty-seventh day of the Expedition on St. Marie soil.'

The brick walls slapped his words back with a flat echo over the still men in uniform. I stood a little behind him, in the shadow of his shoulders, listening. Pel and Moro were behind me.

'I regret to inform you,' Charley said, 'that sniper activity within the City of Blauvain, this day, about thirteen hundred hours, cost us the life of Commander Kensie Graeme.'

There was no sound from the men.

'The snipers have not yet been captured or killed. Since they remain unidentified, Commander Ian Graeme has ordered that the condition of hostilities, which was earlier assumed to have ended, is still in effect. Blauvain has been placed under martial law, sufficient force has been sent to seal the city against any exit or ingress, and all persons under Exotic contract to the Expedition have been recalled to this encampment . . .'

I felt the heat of a breath on my ear and Pel's voice whispered to me.

'Look at them!' he said. 'They're ready to march on Blauvain right now. Do you think they'll let Kensie be killed on some stinking little world like this of ours, and not see that somebody pays for it?'

'Shut up, Pel,' I murmured out of the corner of my mouth at him. But he went on.

'Look at them!' he said. 'It's the order to march they're waiting for – the order to march on Blauvain. And if Charley doesn't end up giving it, there'll be hell to pay. You see how they've all come armed?'

'That's right, Pel, Blauvain's not your city!' It was a bitter whisper from Moro. 'If it was Castelmane they were itching to march on, would you feel the same way about it?'

'Yes!' hissed Pel, fiercely. 'If men come here to risk their lives for us, and we can't do any better than let them be gunned down in the streets, what do we deserve? What does anyone deserve?'

'Stop making a court case out of it!' whispered Moro harshly. 'It's Kensie you're thinking of – that's all. Just like it's only Kensie they're thinking of, out there . . .'

I tried again to quiet them, then realized that actually it did not make any difference. For all practical purposes, the three of us were invisible there behind Charley. The attention of the armed men ranked before us was all on Charley, and only on him. As Pel had said, they were waiting for one certain order; and only that order mattered to them.

It was like standing facing some great, dun-colored, wounded beast which must charge at any second now, if only because in action would there be relief from the pain it was suffering. Charley's expressionless voice went on, each word coming back like a slapping of dry boards together, in the echo from the factory wall. He was issuing a long list of commands having to do with the order of the camp, and its transition back to a condition of battle-alert.

I could feel the tension rising as he approached the end of his list of orders without one which might indicate action by the Expedition against the city in which Kensie had died. Then, suddenly, the list was at an end.

'. . . That concludes,' said Charley, in the same unvarying tones, 'the present orders dealing with the situation. I would remind the personnel of this Expedition that at present the identity of the assassins of Commander Graeme is unknown. The civilian police are exerting every effort to investigate the matter; and it is the opinion of your officers that nothing else can be done for the moment but to give them our complete cooperation. A suspicion exists that a native, outlawed political party, known as The Blue Front, may have been responsible for the assassination. If this should be so, we must be careful to distinguish between those of this world who are actually guilty of Commander Graeme's death and the great majority of innocent bystanders.'

He stopped speaking.

There was not a sound from the thousands of men ranked before him.

'All right, Brigade-Major,' said Charley, looking down from the stand at the ranking officer in the formation. 'Dismiss your troops.'

The Brigade-Major, who had been standing like all the rest facing the stand, wheeled about.

'Atten-shun!' he snapped, and the amplifier sensors of the stand picked his voice up and threw it out over the men in formation as they had projected Charley's voice. 'Dismiss!'

The formation did not disperse. Here and there, a slight wavering in the ranks showed itself, and then the lines of standing figures were motionless again. For a long second, it seemed that nothing more was going to happen, that Charley and the mercenary soldiers before him would

stand facing each other until the day of Judgment . . . and
then somewhere among the ranks, a solitary and off-key
bass voice began to sing.

'They little knew of brotherhood . . .'
Other voices rapidly picked it up.
'. . . The faith of fighting men –
'Who once to prove their lie was good
'Hanged Colonel Jacques Chrétien . . .'

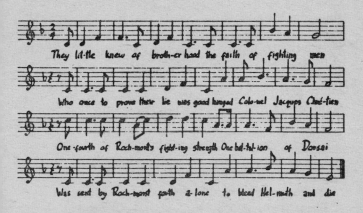

They lit-tle knew of broth-er-hood the faith of fighting men
Who once to prove their lie was good hanged Colo-nel Jacques Chré-tien
One-fourth of Roch-mont's fight-ing strength One bat-tal-ion of Dorsai
Was sent by Roch-mont forth a-lone to bleed Hel-muth and die

– And suddenly they were all singing in the ranks facing
us. It was a song of the young Colonel who had been put to
death one hundred years before, when the Dorsai were
just in their beginning. A New Earth city had employed a
force of Dorsai with the secret intention of using them
against an enemy force so superior as to surely destroy
them utterly – so rendering payment for their services
unnecessary while at the same time doing considerable
damage to the enemy. Then the Dorsai had defeated the
enemy, instead, and the city faced the necessity of paying,
after all. To avoid this, the city authorities came up with
the idea of charging the Dorsai commanding officer with
dealing with the enemy, taking a bribe to claim victory for
a battle never fought at all. It was the technique of the big
lie; and it might even have worked if they had not made

the mistake of arresting the commanding officer, to back up their story.

It was not a song to which I would have had any objection, ordinarily. But now – suddenly – I found it directed at me. It was at Pel, Moro, myself, that the soldiers of the Expedition were all singing it. Before, I had felt almost invisible on the stand behind Charley ap Morgan. Now, we three civilians were the focus of every pair of eyes on the field – we civilians who were like the civilians that had hanged Jacques Chrétien; we who were St. Marians, like whoever had shot Kensie Graeme. It was like facing into the roaring maw of some great beast ready to swallow us up. We stood facing it, frozen.

Nor did Charley ap Morgan interfere.

He stood silent himself, waiting while they went through all the verses of the song to its end: –

. . . *One fourth of Rochmont's fighting strength –*
One battalion of Dorsai –
Was sent by Rochmont forth alone,
To bleed Helmuth, and die.

But look, look down from Rochmont's heights
Upon the Helmuth plain.
At all of Helmuth's armored force
By Dorsai checked, or slain.

Look down, look down, on Rochmont's shame
To hide the wrong she'd done,
Made claim Helmuth had bribed Dorsais –
No battle had been won.

To prove that lie, the Rochmont Lords
Arrested Jacques Chrétien,
On charge he dealt with Helmuth's Chiefs
For payment to his men.

Commandant Arp Van Din sent word:
'You may not judge Dorsai,

132

'Return our Colonel by the dawn,
'Or Rochmont town will die.'

Strong-held behind her walls, Rochmont
Scorned to answer them,
Condemned, and at the daybreak, hanged,
Young Colonel Jacques Chrétien.

Bright, bright, the sun that morning rose
Upon each weaponed wall.
But when the sun set in the west,
Those walls were leveled all.

Then soft and white the moon arose
On streets and roofs unstained,
But when that moon was
*   down once more*
No street nor roof remained.

No more is there a Rochmont town
No more are Rochmont's men.
But stands a Dorsai monument
To Colonel Jacques Chrétien.

So pass the word from world to world,
Alone still stands Dorsai.
But while she lives, no one of hers,
By foreign wrong shall die.

They little knew of brotherhood
– The faith of fighting men –
Who once to prove their lie was good
Hanged Colonel Jacques Chrétien!

It ended. Once more they were silent – utterly silent. On the platform Charley moved. He took half a step forward and the sensors picked up his voice once more and threw it out over the heads of the waiting men.

'Officers! Front and Center. Face your men!'

From the end of each rank figures moved. The commissioned and non-commissioned officers stepped forward, turned and marched to a point opposite the middle of the rank they had headed, turned once more and stood at attention.

'Prepare to fire.'

The weapons in the hands of the officers came up to waist level, their muzzles pointing at the men directly before them. The breath in my chest was suddenly a solid thing. I could not have inhaled or exhaled if I had tried. I had heard of something like this but I had never believed it, let alone dreamed that I would be there to see it happen. Out of the corner of my eye I could see the angle of Charley ap Morgan's face, and it was a Dorsai face in all respects now. He spoke again.

'The command to dismiss has been given,' Charley's voice rang and reechoed over the silent men, 'and not obeyed. The command will be repeated under the stricture of the Third Article of the Professional Soldiers' Covenant. Officers will open fire on any refusing to obey.'

There was something like a small sigh that ran through all the standing men, followed by the faint rattle of safeties being released on the weapons of the men in ranks. They stood facing their officers and non-commissioned officers now – fellow soldiers and old friends. But they were all professionals. They would not simply stand and be executed if it came to the final point. The breath in my chest was now so solid it hurt, like something jagged and heavy pressing against my ribs. In ten seconds we could all be dead.

'Brigade-Major,' said the level voice of Charley. 'Dismiss your troops.'

The Brigade-Major, who had turned once more to face Charley, when Charley spoke to him, turned back again to the parade ground of men.

'Dis –'No more than in Charley's voice was there perceptible change in the Brigade-Major's command from the time it had been given before, '– miss!'

The formations dissolved. All at once the ranks were breaking up, the men in them turning away, the officers and non-coms lowering the weapons they had lifted to ready position at Charley's earlier command. The long-held breath tore itself out of my lungs so roughly it ripped at my throat. I turned to Charley but he was halfway down the steps from the platform, as expressionless as he had been all through the last few minutes. I had to half-run to catch up to him.

'Charley!' I said, reaching him.

He turned to look at me as he walked along. Suddenly I felt how pale and sweat dampened I was. I tried to laugh.

'Thank God that's over,' I said.

'Over?' He shook his head. 'It's not over, Tom. The enlisted men will be voting now. It's their right.'

'Vote?' The world made no sense to me, for a second. Then suddenly it made too much sense. 'You mean – they might vote to march on Blauvain, or something like that?'

'Perhaps – something like that,' he said.

I stared at him.

'And then?' I said. 'You wouldn't . . . if their vote should be to march on Blauvain – what would you do?'

He looked at me almost coldly.

'Lead my troops,' he said.

I stopped. Standing there, I watched him walk away from me. A hand tugged at my elbow; and I turned around to see that Pel and Moro had caught up to me. It was Moro who had his hand on my arm.

'Tom,' said Moro, 'What do we do, now?'

'See Padma,' I said. 'If he can't do something, I don't know anybody who can.'

Charley was not flying directly back to Blauvain. He was already in a staff meeting with his fellow officers, who were barred from the voting of the enlisted men by the Covenant. We three civilians had to borrow a land car from the encampment motor pool.

It was a silent ride, most of the way back into town. Once again I was at the controls, with Pel beside me. Sitting behind us, just before we reached the west area of the city, Moro leaned forward to put his head between us.

135

'Tom,' he said. 'You'll have to put your police on special duty. Pel, you've got to mobilize the militia – right now.'

'Moro,' I answered – and I suddenly felt dog-tired, weary to the point of exhaustion. 'I've got less than three hundred men, ninety-nine per cent of them without anything more exciting in the way of experience than filling out reports or taking charge at a fire, an accident or a family quarrel. They wouldn't face those mercenaries even if I ordered them to.'

'Pel,' he said, turning away from me, 'your men are soldiers. They've been in the field with these mercenaries –'

Pel laughed at him.

'Over a hundred years ago, a battalion of Dorsais took a fortified city – Rochmont – with nothing heavier than light field pieces. This is a *brigade* – six battalions – armed with the best weapons the Exotics can buy them – facing a city with no natural or artificial defenses at all. And you want my two thousand militiamen to try to stop them? There's no force on St. Marie that could stop those professional soldiers.'

'At Rochmont they were all Dorsai –' Moro began.

'For God's sake!' cried Pel. 'These are Dorsai-officered, the best mercenaries you can find. Elite troops – the Exotics don't hire anything else for fear they might have to touch a weapon themselves and damage their enlightenment – or whatever the hell it is! Face it, Moro! If Kensie's troops want to chew us up, they will. And there's nothing you or I can do about it!'

Moro said nothing for a long moment. Pel's last words had hit a near-hysterical note. When the Mayor of Blauvain did speak again, it was softly.

'I just wish to God I knew why you want just that to happen, so badly,' he said.

'Go to hell!' said Pel. 'Just go –'

I slammed the car into retro and we skidded to a halt, thumping down on the grass as the air-cushion quit. I looked at Pel.

'That's something I'd like to know, too,' I said. 'All right, you liked Kensie. So did I. But what we're facing is anything from the leveling of a city to a possible massacre of a couple of hundred thousand people. All that for the death of just one man?'

Pel's face looked bitter and sick.

'We're no good, we St. Marians,' he said, thickly. 'We're a fat little farm world that's never done anything since it was first settled but yell for help to the Exotics every time we got into trouble. And the Exotics have bailed us out every time, only because we're in the same solar system with them. What're we worth? Nothing! At least the Dorsai and the Exotics have got some value – some use!'

He turned away from Moro and myself; and we could not get another word out of him.

We drove on into the city; where, to my great relief, I finally got rid of Pel and Moro both; and was able to get to Police Headquarters and take charge of things.

As I had expected, things badly needed taking care of there. As I should also have expected, I had very much underestimated how badly they needed it. I had planned to spend two or three hours getting the situation under control, and then be free to seek out Padma. But, as it ended up, it took me nearly seven straight hours to damp down the panic, straighten out the confusion, and put some purpose and order back into the operations of all my people, off-duty and otherwise, who had reported for emergency service. Actually, it was little enough we were required to do – merely patrol the streets and see that the town's citizens stayed off the streets and out of the way of the mercenaries. Still, that took seven hours to put into smooth operation; and at the end of that time I was still not free to go hunting for Padma, but had to respond to a series of calls for my presence by the detective crew assigned to work with the mercenaries in tracking down the assassins.

I drove through the empty nighttime streets slowly, with my emergency lights on and the official emblem on my police car clearly illuminated. Three times, however, I was stopped and checked by teams of three to five mercenaries, in battle dress and fully weaponed, that appeared unexpectedly. The third time, the Groupman – a non-commissioned officer – in command of the team stopping me, joined me in the car. When twice after that we encountered military teams, he leaned out the right window to show himself; and we were waved through.

We came at last to a block of warehouses on the north side of the city; and to one warehouse in particular. Within, the large, echoing structure was empty except for a few hundred square feet of crated harvesting machinery on the first of its three floors. I found my men on the second floor in the transparent cubicles that were the building's offices, apparently doing nothing.

'What's the matter?' I said, when I saw them. They were not only idle, but they looked unhappy.

'There's nothing we can do, Superintendent,' said the senior detective lieutenant present – Lee Hall, a man I'd known for sixteen years. 'We can't keep up with them, even if they'd let us.'

'Keep up?' I asked.

'Yes sir,' Lee said. 'Come on, I'll show you. They let us watch, anyway.'

He led me out of the offices up to the top floor of the warehouse, a great, bare space with a few empty crates scattered between piles of unused packing materials. At one end, portable floodlights were illuminating an area with a merciless blue-white light that made the shadows cast by men and things look solid enough to stub your toe on. He led me toward the light until a Groupman stepped forward to bar our way.

'Close enough, Lieutenant,' he said to Lee. He looked at me.

'This is Tomas Velt, Blauvain superintendent of police.'

'Honored to meet you, sir,' said the Groupman to me. 'But you and the Lieutenant will have to stand back here if you want to see what's going on.'

'What is going on?' I asked.

'Reconstruction,' said the Groupman. 'That's one of our Hunter Teams.'

I turned to watch. In the white glare of the light were four of the mercenaries. At first glance they seemed engaged in some odd ballet or mime acting. They were at little distances from one another; and first one, then another of them would move a short distance – perhaps as if he had gotten up from a non-existent chair and walked across to an equally non-existent table, then turned to face the others. Following which another man would move in and apparently do something at the same invisible table with him.

'The men of our Hunter Teams are essentially trackers, Superintendent,' said the Groupman quietly in my ear. 'But some teams are better in certain surroundings than others. These are men of a team that works well in interiors.'

'But what are they doing?' I said.

'Reconstructing what the assassins did when they were here,' said the Groupman. 'Each of three men on the team takes the track of one of the assassins, and the fourth man watches them all as coordinator.'

I looked at him. He wore the sleeve emblem of a Dorsai, but he was as ordinary-looking as myself or one of my detectives. Plainly, a first-generation immigrant to that world; which explained why he was wearing the patches of a non-commissioned, rather than a commissioned officer along with that emblem.

'But what kind of signs are they tracking?' I asked.

'Little things, mostly.' He smiled. 'Tiny things – some things you or I wouldn't be able to see if they were pointed out to us. Sometimes there's nothing and they have to go on guess – that's where the coordinator helps.' He sobered. 'Looks like black magic, doesn't it? It does, even to me, sometimes, and I've been a Dorsai for fourteen years.'

I stared at the moving figures.

'You said – three,' I said.

'That's right,' answered the Groupman. 'There were three snipers. We've tracked them from the office in the building they fired from, to here. This was their headquarters – the place they moved from, to the office, just before the killing. There's sign they were here a couple of days, at least, waiting.'

'Waiting?' I asked. 'How do you know there were three and they were waiting?'

'Lots of repetitive sign. Habitual actions. Signs of camping beds set up. Food signs for a number of meals. Metal lubricant signs showing weapons had been disassembled and worked over here. Signs of a portable, private phone – they must have waited for a phone call from someone telling them the Commander was on his way in from the encampment.'

'But how do you know there were only three?'

'There's sign for only three,' he said. 'Three – all big for your world, all under thirty. The biggest man had black hair and a full beard. He was the one who hadn't changed clothes for a week –' The Groupman sniffed the air. 'Smell him?'

I sniffed hard and long.

'I don't smell a thing,' I said.

'Hmm,' the Groupman looked grimly pleased. 'Maybe those fourteen years have done me some good, after all. The stink of him's in the air, all right. It's one of the things our Hunter Teams followed to this place.'

I looked aside at Lee Hall, then back at the soldier.

'You don't need my detectives at all, do you?' I said.

'No sir,' he looked me in the face. 'But we assume you'd want them to stay with us. That's all right.'

'Yes,' I said. And I left there. If my men were not needed, neither was I; and I had no time to stand around being useless. There was still Padma to talk to.

But it was not easy to locate the Outbond. The Exotic Embassy either could not or would not tell me where he was; and the Expedition Headquarters in Blauvain also claimed not to know. As a matter of ordinary police work, my own department kept track of important outworlders like the Graeme brothers and the Outbond, as they moved around our city. But in this case, there was no record of Padma ever leaving the room in which I had last seen him with Ian Graeme, early in the day. I finally took my determination in both hands and called Ian himself to ask if Padma was with him.

The answer was a blunt 'no'. That settled it. If Padma was with him, a dorsai like Ian would have refused to answer rather than lie outright. I gave up. I was light-headed with fatigue and I told myself I would go home, get at least a few hours' sleep, and then try again.

So, with one of the professional soldiers in my police car to vouch for me at roadblocks, I returned to my own dark apartment; and when, alone at last, I came into the living room and turned on the light, there was Padma waiting for me in one of my own chair-floats.

The jar of finding him there was solid – more like an emotional explosion than I would have thought. It was like seeing a ghost in reality, the ghost of someone from whose funeral you have just returned. I stood staring at him.

'Sorry to startle you, Tom,' he said. 'I know, you were going to have a drink and forget about everything for a few hours. Why don't you have the drink, anyway?'

He nodded toward the bar built into a corner of the apartment living room. I never used the thing unless there were guests on hand; but it was always stocked – that was part of the maintenance agreement in the lease. I went over and punched the buttons for a single brandy and water. I knew there was no use offering Padma alcohol.

'How did you get in here?' I said, with my back to him.

'I told your supervisor you were looking for me,' Padma said. 'He let me in. We Exotics aren't so common on your world here that he didn't recognize me.'

I swallowed half the glass at a gulp, carried the drink

141

back, and sat down in a chair opposite him. The background lighting in the apartment had gone on automatically when night darkened the windows. It was a soft light, pouring from the corners of the ceiling and from little random apertures and niches in the walls. Under it, in his blue robe, with his ageless face, Padma looked like the image of a buddha, beyond all the human and ordinary storms of life.

'What are you doing here?' I asked. 'I've been looking all over for you.'

'That's why I'm here,' Padma said. 'The situation being what it is, you would want to appeal to me to help you with it. So I wanted to see you away from any place where you might blame my refusal to help on outside pressures.'

'Refusal?' I said. It was probably my imagination; but the brandy and water I had swallowed seemed to have gone to my head already. I felt light-minded and unreal. 'You aren't even going to listen to me first before saying no?'

'My hope,' said Padma, 'is that you'll listen to me, first, Tom, before rejecting what I've got to tell you. You're thinking that I could bring pressure to bear on Ian Graeme to move his soldiers half a world away from Blauvain, or otherwise take the situation out of its critical present phase. But the truth is I could not; and even if I could, I would not.'

'Would not,' I echoed, muzzily.

'Yes. Would not. But not just because of personal choice. For four centuries now, Tom, we students of the Exotic Sciences have been telling other men and women that our human race was committed to a future, to the workings of history as it is. It's true we Exotics have a calculative technique now, called ontogenetics, that helps us to resolve any present or predicted moment into its larger historical factors. We've made no secret of having such techniques. But that doesn't mean we can control what will happen, particularly while other men still tend to reject the very thing we work with – the concept of a large, shifting pattern of events that involves all of us and our lives.'

'I'm a Catholic,' I said. 'I don't believe in predestination.'

'Neither do we on Mara and Kultis,' said Padma. 'But we do believe in a physics of human action and inter-action, which we believe works in a certain direction, toward a certain goal which we now think is less than a hundred years off – if, in fact, we haven't already reached it. Movement toward that goal has been building up for at least the last thousand years; and by now the momentum of its forces is massive. No single individual or group of individuals at the present time have the mass to oppose or turn that movement from its path. Only something greater than a human being as we know a human being might do that.'

'Sure,' I said. The glass in my hand was empty. I did not remember drinking the rest of its contents; but the alcohol was bringing me a certain easing of weariness and tension. I got up, went back to the bar, and came back with a full glass, while Padma waited silently. 'Sure, I understand. You think you've spotted a historical trend here; and you don't want to interfere for fear of spoiling it. A fancy excuse to do nothing.'

'Not an excuse, Tom,' Padma said; and there was some-thing different, like a deep gong-note in his voice, that blew the fumes of the brandy clear from my wits for a second and made me look at him. 'I'm not telling you I won't do anything about the situation. I'm telling you that I can't do anything about it. Even if I tried to do some-thing, it would be no use. It's not for you alone that the situation is too massive; it's that way for everyone.'

'How do you know if you don't try?' I said. 'Let me see you try, and it not work. Then maybe I'd believe you.'

'Tom,' he said, 'can you lift me out of this chair?'

I blinked at him. I am no Dorsai, as I think I have said, but I am large for my world, which meant in this case that I was a head taller than Padma and perhaps a quarter again the weight. Also I was undoubtedly younger; and I had

143

worked all my life to stay in good physical condition. I could have lifted someone my own weight out of that chair with no trouble, and Padma was less than that.

'Unless you're tied down,' I said.

'I'm not.' He stood up briefly, and then sat again. 'Try and lift me, Tom.'

I put my glass down, stepped over to his float and stood behind him. I wrapped my arms around his body under his armpits, and lifted – at first easily, then with all my strength.

But not only could I not lift him, I could not budge him. If he had been a lifesized statue of stone I would have expected to feel more reaction and movement in response to my efforts.

I gave up finally, panting, and stood back from him.

'What do you weigh?' I demanded.

'No more than you think. Sit down again, Tom –' I did. 'Don't let it bother you. It's a trick, of course. No, not a mechanical trick, a physiological one – but a trick just the same, that's been shown on stage at times, at least during the last four hundred years.'

'Stand up,' I said. 'Let me try again.'

He did. I did. He was still immovable.

'Now,' he said, when I had given up a second time. 'Try once more; and you'll find you can lift me.'

I wiped my forehead, put my arms around him, and heaved upward with all my strength. I almost threw him against the ceiling overhead. Numbly I set him down again.

'You see?' he said, reseating himself. 'Just as I knew you could not lift me until I let you, I know that there is nothing I can do to alter present events here on St. Marie from their present direction. But you can.'

'*I* can?' I stared at him, then exploded. 'Then for God's sake tell me how?'

He shook his head, slowly.

'I'm sorry, Tom,' he said. 'But that's just what I can't do. I only know that, resolved to ontogenetic terms, the situation here shows you as a pivotal character. On you, as a point, the bundle of human forces that were concentrated here and bent toward destruction by another such pivotal character, may be redirected back into the general historical pattern with a minimum of harm. I tell you this so that being aware of it, you can be watching for opportunities to redirect. That's all I can do.'

Incredibly, with those words, he got up and went toward the door of the apartment.

'Hold on!' I said, and he stopped, turning back momentarily. 'This other pivotal character. Who's he?'

Padma shook his head again.

'It would do you no good to know,' he said. 'I give you my word he is now far away from the situation and will not be coming back to it. He is not even on the planet.'

'One of the assassins of Kensie!' I said. 'And they've gotten away, off-planet!'

'No,' said Padma. 'No. The men who assassinated Kensie are only tools of events. If none of them had existed, three others would have been there in their place. Forget this other pivotal character, Tom. He was no more in charge of the situation he created than you are in charge of the situation here and now. He was simply, like you, in a position that gave him freedom of choice. Good night.'

With those last words, he was suddenly out the door and gone. To this day I cannot remember if he moved particularly swiftly; or whether for some reason I now can't remember I simply let him go. Just – all at once I was alone.

Fatigue rolled over me like the heavy waves of some ocean of mercury. I stumbled into the bedroom, fell on my sleeping float, and that was all I remembered until – only a second later, it seemed – I woke to the hammering of my telephone's chimes on my ears.

I reached out, fumbled at the bedside table and pushed the *on* button.

'Velt here,' I said, thickly.

'Tom – this is Moro. Tom? Is that you, Tom?'

145

I licked my lips, swallowed and spoke more understandably.

'It's me,' I said. 'What's the call for?'

'Where've you been?'

'Sleeping,' I said. 'What's the call for?'

'I've got to talk to you. Can you come –'

'You come here,' I said. 'I've got to get up and dress and get some coffee in me before I go anyplace. You can talk to me while I'm doing it.'

I punched off. He was still saying something at the other end of the line but just then I did not care what it was.

I pushed my dead-heavy body out of bed and began to move. I was dressed and at the coffee when he came.

'Have a cup.' I pushed it at him as he sat down at the porch table with me. He took it automatically.

'Tom – ' he said. The cup trembled in his hand as he lifted it and he sipped hastily from it before putting it down again. 'Tom, you were in the Blue Front once, weren't you?'

'Weren't we all?' I said. 'Back when we and it were young together; and it was an idealistic outfit aimed at putting some order and system into our world government?'

'Yes, yes of course,' Moro said. 'But what I mean is, if you were a member once, maybe you know who to contact now –'

I began to laugh. I laughed so hard I had to put my cup down to avoid spilling it.

'Moro, don't you know better than that?' I said. 'If I knew who the present leaders of the Blue Front were, they'd be in jail. The Blauvain police commissioner – the head law enforcement man of our capital city – is the last man the Blue Front would be in touch with nowadays. They'd come to you, first. You were a member once, too, back in college days, remember?'

'Yes,' he said miserably. 'But I don't know anything now, just as you're saying. I thought you might have informers, or suspicions you couldn't prove, or –'

'None of them,' I said. 'All right. Why do you want to

146

know who's running the Blue Front, now?'

'I thought I'd make an appeal to them, to give up the assassins of Kensie Graeme – to save the Blauvain people. Tom –' he stared directly at me. 'Just an hour ago the enlisted men of the mercenaries took a vote on whether to demand their officers lead them on the city. They voted, over ninety-four per cent, in favor. And Pel . . . Pel's finally mobilized his militia; but I don't think he means to help *us*. He's been trying to get in to talk to Ian all day.'

'All day?' I glanced at the time on my wrist unit. '4:25 – it's not 4:25 pm, *now*?'

'Yes,' said Moro, staring at me. 'I thought you knew.'

'I didn't mean to sleep like this!' I came out of the chair, moving toward the door. 'Pel's trying to see Ian? The sooner we get down and see him ourselves, the better.'

So we went. But we were too late. By the time we got to Expedition Headquarters and past the junior officers to the door of the office where Ian was, Pel was already with Ian. I brushed aside the Force Leader barring our way and walked in, followed by Moro. Pel was standing facing Ian, who sat at a desk surrounded by stacks of filmprints. He got to his feet as Moro and I appeared.

'That'll be all right, Force-Leader,' he said to the officer behind us. 'Tom, I'm glad you're here. Mr. Mayor, though, if you don't mind waiting outside, I'll see you in a few minutes.'

Moro had little choice but to go out again. The door shut behind him, Ian waved me to a chair beside Pel, and sat down again himself.

'Go ahead, General,' he said to Pel. 'Repeat what you'd started to tell me, for the benefit of Tom, here.'

Pel glanced savagely at me for a second out of the edge of his eyes before answering.

'This doesn't have anything to do with the Police Commissioner of Blauvain,' he said, 'or anyone else of St. Marie.'

'Repeat,' said Ian again. He did not raise his voice. The word was simply an iron door dropped in Pel's way, forcing him to turn back. Pel glanced once more, grimly, at me.

'I was just saying,' he said, 'if Commander Graeme would go to the encampment and speak to the enlisted men there, he could probably get them to vote unanimously.'

'Vote unanimously for what?' I asked.

'For a house-to-house search of the Blauvain area,' Ian answered.

'The city's been cordoned,' Pel said quickly. 'A search like that would turn up the assassins in a matter of hours, with the whole expeditionary force searching.'

'Sure,' I said, 'and with the actual assassins, there'd be a few hundred suspected assassins, or people who fought or ran for the wrong reason, killed or wounded by the searchers. Even if the Blue Front didn't take advantage of the opportunity – which they certainly would – to start gunfights with the soldiers in the city streets.'

'What of it?' said Pel, talking to Ian rather than to me. 'Your troops can handle any Blue Front people. And you'd be doing St. Marie a favor to wipe them out.'

'If the whole thing didn't develop into a wiping-out of the whole civilian population of the city,' I said.

'You're implying, Tom,' said Pel, 'that the Exotic troops can't be controlled by –'

Ian cut him short.

'Your suggestion, General,' he said, 'is the same one I've been getting from other quarters. Someone else is here with it right now. I'll let you listen to the answer I give him.'

He turned toward his desk annunciator.

'Send in Groupman Whallo,' he said.

He straightened up and turned back to us as the door to his office opened and in came the mercenary noncom I had brushed past out there. In the light, I saw it was the immigrant Dorsai of the Hunter Team I had encountered – the man who had been a Dorsai fourteen years.

'Sir!' he said, stopping a few steps before Ian and saluting. Uncovered himself, Ian did not return the salute.

'You've got a message for me?' Ian said. 'Go ahead. I want these gentlemen to hear it, and my answer.'

'Yes, sir,' said Whallo. I could see him glance at and recognize me out of the corner of his eye. 'As representative of the enlisted men of the Expedition, I have been sent to convey to you the results of our latest vote on orders. By unanimous vote, the enlisted men of this command have concurred in the need for a single operation.'

'Which is?'

'That a house-to-house search of the Blauvain city area be made for the assassins of Field Commander Graeme,' said Whallo. He nodded at Ian's desk and for the first time I saw solidigraphs there – artists' impressions, undoubtedly, but looking remarkably lifelike of three men in civilian clothes. 'There's no danger we won't recognize them when we find them.'

Whallo's formal and artificial delivery was at odds with the way I had heard him speak when I had run into him at the Hunter Team site. There was, it occurred to me suddenly, probably a military protocol even to matters like this – even to the matter of a man's death and the possible death of a city. It came as a little shock to realize it and for the first time I began to feel something of what Padma had meant in saying that the momentum of forces involved here was massive. For a second it was almost as if I could feel those forces like great winds, blowing on the present moment. But Ian was already answering him.

'Any house-to-house search involves possible military errors and danger to the civilian population,' he was saying. 'The military record of my brother is not to be marred after his death by any intemperate order from me.'

'Yes sir,' said Whallo. 'I'm sorry sir; but the enlisted men of the expedition had hoped that the action would be ordered by you. Their decision calls for six hours in which you may consider the matter before our Enlisted Men's Council takes the responsibility for the action upon itself. Meanwhile, the Hunter Teams will be withdrawn – this is part of the voted decision.'

149

'That, too?' said Ian.

'I'm sorry, sir. But you know,' said Whallo, 'they've been at a dead end for some hours now. The trail was lost in traffic; and the men might be anywhere in the central part of the city. '

'Yes,' said Ian. 'Well, thank you for your message, Groupman.'

'Sir!' said Whallo. He saluted again and went out.

As the door closed behind him, Ian's head turned back to face Pel and myself.

'You heard, gentlemen,' he said. 'Now, I've got work to do.'

Pel and I left. In the corridor outside, Whallo was already gone and the young Force-Leader was absent. Only Moro stood waiting for us. Pel turned on me, furiously.

'Who asked you to show up here?' he demanded.

'Moro,' I answered. 'And a good thing, too. Pel, what's got into you? You act as if you had some personal axe to grind in seeing the Exotic mercenaries level Blauvain –'

He spun away from me.

'Excuse me!' he snapped. 'I've got things to do. I've got to phone my Headquarters.'

Puzzled, I watched him take a couple of long strides away from me and out of the outer office. Suddenly, it was as if the winds of those massive forces I had felt for a moment just past in Ian's office had blown my head strangely clean, clear and empty, so that the slightest sound echoed with importance. All at once, I was hearing the echo of Pel saying those identical words as Kensie was preparing to leave the mercenary encampment for the non-existent victory dinner; and a half-recognized but long-held suspicion in me flared into a raging certainty.

I took three long strides after him and caught him. I whirled him around and rammed him up against a wall.

'It was you!' I said. 'You called from the Encampment to the city just before we drove in. It was you who told the assassins we were on the way and to move into position to snipe at our car. You're Blue Front, Pel; and you set Kensie up to be murdered!'

My hands were on his throat and he could not have answered if he had wanted to. But he did not need to. Then I heard the click of bootheels on the floor of the polished stone corridor flagging outside the office, and let go of him, slipping my hand under my uniform jacket to my beltgun.

'Say a word,' I whispered to him, 'or try anything . . . and I'll kill you before you can get the first syllable out. You're coming along with us!'

The Force-Leader entered. He glanced at the three of us curiously.

'Something I can do for you gentlemen?' he asked.

'No,' I said, 'No, we're just leaving.'

With one arm through Pel's and the hand of my other arm under my jacket on the butt of my beltgun, we went out as close as the old friends we had always been, Moro bringing up the rear. Out in the corridor, with the office door behind us, Moro caught up with me on the opposite side from Pel.

'What are we going to do?' Moro whispered. Pel had still said nothing; but his eyes were like the black shadows of meteor craters on the gray face of an airless moon.

'Take him downstairs and out to a locked room in the nearest police post,' I said. 'He's a walking stick of high explosive if any of the mercenaries find out what he did. Someone of his rank involved in Kensie's killing is all the excuse they need to run our streets red in the gutters.'

We got Pel to a private back room in Post Ninety-six, a local police center less than three minutes' drive from the building where Ian had his office.

'But how can you be sure, he –' Moro hesitated at putting it into words, once we were safe in the room. He stood staring at Pel, who sat huddled in a chair, still without speaking.

'I'm sure,' I said. 'The Exotic, Padma –' I cut myself off

as much as Moro had done. 'Never mind. The main thing is he's Blue Front, he's involved – and what do we do about it?'

Pel stirred and spoke for the first time since I had almost strangled him. He looked up at Moro and myself out of his grey-dead face.

'I did it for St. Marie!' he said, hoarsely. 'But I didn't know they were going to kill him! I didn't know that. They said it was just to be shooting around the car – for an incident –'

'You hear?' I jerked my head at Moro. 'Do you want more proof than that?'

'What'll we do?' Moro was staring in fascinated horror at Pel.

'That was my question,' I reminded him. He stood there looking hardly in better case than Pel. 'But it doesn't look like you're going to be much help in answering it.' I laughed, but not happily. 'Padma said the choice was up to me.'

'Who? What're you talking about? What choice?' asked Moro.

'Pel here –' I nodded at him, 'knows where the assassins are hiding.'

'No,' said Pel.

'Well, you know enough so that we can find them,' I said. 'It makes no difference. And outside of this room, there're only two people on St. Marie we can trust with that information.'

'You think I'd tell you anything?' Pel said. His face was still grey, but it had firmed up now. 'Do you think even if I knew anything I'd tell you? St. Marie needs a strong government to survive and only the Blue Front can give it to her. I was ready to give my life for that, yesterday. I'm still willing. I won't tell you anything – and you can't make me. Not in six hours.'

'What two people?' Moro asked me.

'Padma,' I said, 'and Ian.'

'Ian!' said Pel. 'You think he'll help you? He doesn't

152

give a damn for St. Marie, either way. Did you believe that talk of his about his brother's military record? He's got no feelings. It's his own military record he's concerned with; and he doesn't care if the mercenaries tear Blauvain up by the roots, as long as it's done over his own objection. He's just as happy as any of the other mercenaries with that vote. He's just going to sit out his six hours and let things happen.'

'And I suppose Padma doesn't care either?' Moro was beginning to sound a little ugly himself. 'It was the Exotics sent us help against the Friendlies in the first place!'

'Who knows what Exotics want?' Pel retorted. 'They pretend to go about doing nothing but helping other people, and never dirtying their hands with violence and so on; and somehow with all that they keep on getting richer and more powerful all the time. Sure, trust Padma, why don't you? Trust Padma and see what happens!'

Moro looked at me uncomfortably.

'What if he's right?' Moro said.

'What if he's right?' I snarled at him. 'Moro, can't you see this is what St. Marie's trouble has always been? Here's the troublemaker we always have around – someone like Pel – whispering that the devil's in the chimney and you – like the rest of our people always do – starting to shake at the knees and wanting to sell him the house at any price! Stay here both of you; and don't try to leave the room.'

I went out, locking the door behind me. They were in one of a number of rooms set up behind the duty officer's desk and I went up to the night sergeant on duty. He was a man I'd known back when I had been in detective training on the Blauvain force, an old-line policeman named Jaker Reales.

'Jaker,' I said, 'I've got a couple of valuable items locked up in that back room. I hope to be back in an hour or so to collect them; but if I don't, make sure they don't get out and nobody gets in to them, or knows they're there. I don't care what kind of noises may seem to come

153

out of there, it's all in the imagination of anyone who thinks he hears them, for twenty-four hours at least, if I don't come back.'

'Got you, Tom,' said Jaker. 'Leave it up to me, sir.'

'Thanks, Jaker,' I said.

I went out and back to Expedition Headquarters. It had not occurred to me to wonder what Ian would do now that his Hunter Teams had been taken from him. I found Expedition Headquarters now quietly aswarm with officers – officers who clearly were most of them Dorsai. No enlisted men were to be seen.

I was braced to argue my way into seeing Ian; but the men on duty surprised me. I had to wait only four or five minutes outside the door of Ian's private office before six Senior Commandants, Charley ap Morgan among them, filed out.

'Good,' said Charley, nodding as he saw me; and then went on without any further explanation of what he meant. I had no time even to look after him. Ian was waiting.

I went in. Ian sat massively behind his desk, waiting for me, and waved me to a chair facing him as I came in. I sat down. He was only a few feet from me, but again I had the feeling of a vast distance separating us. Even here and now, under the soft lights of this nighttime office, he conveyed, more strongly than any Dorsai I had ever seen, a sense of difference. Generations of men bred to war had made him; and I could not warm to him as Pel and others had warmed to Kensie. Far from kindling any affection in me, as he sat there, a cold wind like that off some icy and barren mountaintop seemed to blow from him to me, chilling me. I could believe Pel, that Ian was all ice and no blood; and there was no reason for me to do anything for him – except that as a man whose brother had been killed, he deserved whatever help any other decent, law-abiding man could give him.

But I owed something to myself, too, and to the fact that we were not all villains, like Pel, on St. Marie.

154

'I've got something to tell you,' I said. 'It's about General Sinjin.'

He nodded, slowly.

'I've been waiting for you to come to me with that,' he said.

I stared at him.

'You knew about Pel?' I said.

'We knew someone from the St. Marie authorities had to be involved in what happened,' he said. 'Normally, a Dorsai officer is alert to any potentially dangerous situation. But there was the false dinner invitation; and then the matter of the assassins happening to be in just the right place at the right time, with just the right weapons. Also, our Hunter Teams found clear evidence the encounter was no accident. As I say, an officer like Field Commander Graeme is not ordinarily killed that easily.'

It was odd to sit there and hear him speak Kensie's name that way. Title and name rang on my ears with the strangeness one feels when somebody speaks of himself in the third person.

'But Pel?' I said.

'We didn't know it was General Sinjin who was involved,' Ian said. 'You identified him yourself by coming to me about him just now.'

'He's Blue Front,' I said.

'Yes,' said Ian, nodding.

'I've known him all my life,' I said, carefully. 'I believe he's suffered some sort of nervous breakdown over the death of your brother. You know, he admired your brother very much. But he's still the man I grew up with; and that man can't be easily made to do something he doesn't want to do. Pel says he won't tell us anything that'll help us find the assassins; and he doesn't think we can make him tell us inside of the six hours left before your soldiers move in to search Blauvain. Knowing him, I'm afraid he's right.'

I stopped talking. Ian sat where he was, behind the desk, looking at me, merely waiting.

'Don't you understand?' I said. 'Pel can help us, but I don't know of any way to make him do it.'

Still Ian said nothing.

'What do you want from me?' I almost shouted it at him, at last.

'Whatever,' Ian said, 'you have to give.'

For a moment it seemed to me that there was something like a crack in the granite mountain that he seemed to be. For a moment I could have sworn that I saw into him. But if this was true, the crack closed up immediately, the minute I glimpsed it. He sat remote, icy, waiting, there behind his desk.

'I've got nothing,' I said, 'unless you know of some way to make Pel talk.'

'I have no way consistent with my brother's reputation as a Dorsai officer,' said Ian, remotely.

'You're concerned with reputations?' I said. 'I'm concerned with the people who'll die and be hurt in Blauvain if your mercenaries come in to hunt door-to-door for those assassins. Which is more important, the reputation of a dead man, or the lives of living ones?'

'The people are rightly your concern, Commissioner,' said Ian, still remotely, 'the professional reputation of Kensie Graeme is rightly mine.'

'What will happen to that reputation if those troops move into Blauvain in less than six hours from now?' I demanded.

'Something not good,' Ian said. 'That doesn't change my personal responsibilities. I can't do what I shouldn't do and I must do what I ought to do.'

I stood up.

'There's no answer to the situation, then,' I said. Suddenly, the utter tiredness I had felt before was on me again. I was tired of the fanatic Friendlies who had come out of another solar system to exercise a purely theoretical claim to our revenues and world surface as an excuse to assault St. Marie. I was tired of the Blue Front and people like Pel. I was tired of offworld people of all

156

kinds, including Exotics and Dorsais. I was tired, tired
. . . It came to me then that I could walk out. I could
refuse to make the decision that Padma had said I would
make and the whole matter would be out of my hands. I
told myself to do that, to get up and walk out; but my
feet did not budge. In picking on me, events had chosen
the right idiot as a pivot point. Like Ian, I could not do
what I should not do, and I must do what I ought to do.

'All right,' I said, 'Padma might be able to do something with him.'

'The Exotics,' said Ian, 'force nobody.' But he stood up.

'Maybe I can talk him into it,' I said, exhaustedly. 'At
least, I can try.'

Once more, I would have had no idea where to find
Padma in a hurry. But Ian located him in a research
enclosure, a carrel in the stacks of the Blauvain library;
which like many libraries on all the eleven inhabited
worlds, had been Exotic-endowed. In the small space of
the carrel Ian and I faced him; the two of us standing,
Padma seated in the serenity of his blue robe and
unchanging facial expression. I told him what we needed
with Pel, and he shook his head.

'Tom,' he said, 'you must already know that we who
study the Exotic sciences never force anyone or anything.
Not for moral reasons alone; but because using force
would damage our ability to do the sensitive work we've
dedicated our lives to doing. That's why we hire
mercenaries to fight for us, and Cetan lawyers to handle
our off-world business contracts. I am the last person on
this world to make Pel talk.'

'Don't you feel any responsibility to the innocent
people of this city?' I said. 'To the lives that will be lost if
he doesn't?'

'Emotionally, yes,' Padma said, softly. 'But there are
practical limits to the responsibility of personal inaction.
If I were to concern myself with all possible pain conse-
quent upon the least, single action of mine, I would have
to spend my life like a statue. I was not responsible for

157

Kensie's death; and I am not responsible for finding his killers. Without such a responsibility I can't violate the most basic prohibition of my life's rules.'

'You knew Kensie,' I said. 'Don't you owe anything to him? And don't you owe anything to the same St. Marie people you sent an armed expedition to help?'

'We make it a point to give, rather than take,' Padma said, 'just to avoid debts like that which could force us into doing what we shouldn't do. No, Tom. The Exotics and I have no obligation to your people, or even to Kensie.'

'– And to the Dorsai?' asked Ian, behind me.

I had almost forgotten he was there, I had been concentrating so hard on Padma. Certainly, I had not expected Ian to speak. The sound of his deep voice was like a heavy bell tolling in the small room; and for the first time Padma's face changed.

'The Dorsai . . .' he echoed. 'Yes, the time is coming when there will be neither Exotics nor Dorsai, in the end when the final development is achieved. But we Exotics have always counted on our work as a step on the way to that end; and the Dorsai helped us up our step. Possibly, if things had gone otherwise, the Dorsai might have never been; and we would still be where we are now. But things went as they have; and our thread has been tangled with the Dorsai thread from the time your many-times removed grandfather Cletus Grahame first freed all the younger worlds from the politics of Earth . . .'

He stood up.

'I'll force no one,' he said. 'But I will offer Pel my help to find peace with himself, if he can; and if he finds such peace, then maybe he will want to tell you willingly what you want to know.'

Padma, Ian and I went back to the police station where I had left Pel and Moro locked up. We let Moro out, and closed the door upon the three of us with Pel. He sat in a chair, looking at us, pale, pinch-faced and composed.

'So you brought the Exotic, did you, Tom?' he said to

me. 'What's it going to be? Some kind of hypnosis?'

'No, Pel,' said Padma softly, pacing across the room to him as Ian and I sat down to wait. 'I would not deal in hypnosis, particularly without the consent of the one to be hypnotized.'

'Well, you sure as hell haven't got my consent!' said Pel.

Padma had reached him now and was standing over him. Pel looked up into the calm face above the blue robe.

'But try it if you like.' Pel said, 'I don't hypnotize easily.'

'No,' said Padma. 'I've said I would not hypnotize anyone; but in any case, neither you nor anyone else can be hypnotized without his or her innate consent. All things between individuals are done by consent. The prisoner consents to his captivity as the patient consents to his surgery – the difference is only in degree and pattern. The great, blind mass that is humanity in general is like an amoebic animal. It exists by internal laws that cohere its body and its actions. Those internal laws are based upon conscious and unconscious, mutual consents of its atoms – ourselves – to work with each other and cooperate. Peace and satisfaction come to each of us in proportion to our success in such cooperation, in the forward-searching movement of the humanity-creature as a whole. Non-consent and noncooperation work against the grain. Pain and self-hate result from friction when we fight against our natural desire to cooperate . . .'

His voice went on. Gently but compellingly he said a great deal more, and I understood all at the time; but beyond what I have quoted so far – and those first few sentences stay printed-clear in my memory – I do not recall another specific word. I do not know to this day what happened. Perhaps I half-dozed without realizing I was dozing. At any rate, time passed; and when I reached a point where the memory record took up again, he was leaving and Pel had altered.

'I can talk to you some more, can't I?' Pel said as the Outbond rose to leave. Pel's voice had become clear-toned and strangely young-sounding. 'I don't mean now. I mean, there'll be other times?'

'I'm afraid not,' Padma said. 'I'll have to leave St. Marie shortly. My work takes me back to my own world and then on to one of the Friendly planets to meet someone and wind up what began here. But you don't need me to talk to. You created your own insights as we talked, and you can go on doing that by yourself. Goodby, Pel.'

'Goodby,' said Pel. He watched Padma leave. When he looked at me again his face, like his voice, was clear and younger than I had seen it in years. 'Did you hear all that, Tom?'

'I think so . . .' I said; because already the memory was beginning to slip away from me. I could feel the import of what Padma had said to Pel, but without being able to give it exact shape, it was as if I had intercepted a message that had turned out to be not for me, and so my mental machinery had already begun to cancel it out. I got up and went over to Pel. 'You'll help us find those assassins, now?'

'Yes,' he said. 'Of course I will.'

He was able to give us a list of five places that were possible hiding places for the three we hunted. He provided exact directions for finding each one.

'Now,' I said to Ian, when Pel was through, 'we need those Hunter Teams of yours that were pulled off.'

'We have Hunters,' said Ian. 'Those officers who are Dorsai are still with us; and there are Hunters among them.'

He stepped to the phone unit on the desk in the room and put a call in to Charley ap Morgan, at Expeditionary Headquarters. When Charley answered, Ian gave him the five locations Pel had supplied us.

'Now,' he said to me as he turned away from the phone. 'We'll go back to my office.'

'I want to come,' said Pel. Ian looked at him for a long

moment, then nodded, without changing expression.

'You can come,' he said.

When we got back to the Expeditionary Headquarters building, the rooms and corridors there seemed even more aswarm with officers. As Ian had said, they were mostly Dorsai. But I saw some among them who might not have been. Apparently Ian commanded his own loyalty, or perhaps it was the Dorsai concept that commanded its own loyalty to whoever was commanding officer. We went to his office; and, sitting there, waited while the reports began to come in.

The first three locations to be checked out by the officer Hunter Teams drew blanks. The fourth showed evidence of having been used within the last twenty-four hours, although it was empty now. The last location to be checked also drew blank.

The Hunter Teams concentrated on the fourth location and began to work outward from it, hoping to cross sign of a trail away from it. I checked the clock figures on my wrist unit. It was now nearing one a.m. in the morning, local time; and the six hour deadline of the enlisted mercenaries was due to expire in forty-seven minutes. In the office where I waited with Ian, Pel, Charley ap Morgan, and another senior Dorsai officer, the air was thick with the tension of waiting. Ian and the two other Dorsai sat still; even Pel sat still. I was the one who fidgeted and paced, as the time continued to run out.

The phone on Ian's desk flashed its visual signal light. Ian reached out to punch it on.

'Yes?' he said.

'Hunter Team Three,' said a voice from the desk. 'We have clear sign and are following now. Suggest you join us, sir.'

'Thank you. Coming,' said Ian.

We went, Ian, Charley, Pel and myself, in an Expedition Command Car. It was an eerie ride through the patrolled and deserted streets of my city. Ian's Hunter Team Three was ahead of us and led us to an apartment hotel on the upper north side of the city, in the oldest section.

The building had been built of poured cement faced with Castlemane granite. Inside, the corridors were old-fashionedly narrow and close-feeling, with dark, thick carpeting and metal walls in imitation oak woodgrain. The soundproofing was good, however. We mounted to the seventh story and moved down the hall to suite number 415 without hearing any sound other than those we made, ourselves.

'Here,' finally said the leader of the Hunter Team, a lean, gnarled Dorsai Senior Commandant in his late fifties. He gestured to the door of 415. 'All three of them.'

'Ian,' said Charley ap Morgan, glancing at his wrist unit. 'The enlisted men start moving into the city in six minutes. You could go meet them to say we've found the assassins. The others and I –'

'No,' said Ian. 'We can't say we've found them until we see them and identify them positively.' He stepped up to one side of the door; and, reaching out an arm, touched the door annunciator stud.

There was no response. Above the door, the half-meter square annunciator screen stayed brown and blank.

Ian pressed the button again.

Again we waited, and there was no response.

Ian pressed the stud. Holding it down, so that his voice would go with the sound of its announcing chimes to the ears of those within, he spoke.

'This is Commander Ian Graeme,' he said. 'Blauvain is now under martial law; and you are under arrest in connection with the assassination of Field Commander Kensie Graeme. If necessary, we can cut our way in to you. However, I'm concerned that Field Commander Graeme's reputation be kept free of criticism in the matter of determining responsibility for his death. So I'm offering you the chance to come out and surrender.'

He released the stud and stopped talking. There was a long pause. Then a voice spoke from the annunciator grille below the screen, although the screen itself remained blank.

'Go to hell, Graeme,' said the voice. 'We got your brother; and if you try to blast your way in here, we'll get you, too.'

'My advice to you,' said Ian – his voice was cold, distant, and impersonal, as if this was something he did every day, 'is to surrender.'

'You guarantee our safety if we do?'

'No,' said Ian. 'I only guarantee that I will see that Field Commander Graeme's reputation is not adversely affected by the way you're handled.'

There was no immediate answer from the screen. Behind Ian, Charley looked again at his wrist unit.

'They're playing for time,' he said. 'But why? What good will that do them?'

'They're fanatics,' said Pel, softly. 'Just as much fanatics as the Friendly soldiers were, only for the Blue Front instead of for some puritan form of religion. Those three in there don't expect to get out of this alive. They're only trying to set a higher price on their own deaths – get something more for their dying.'

Charley ap Morgan's wrist unit chimed.

'Time's up,' he said to Ian. 'The enlisted men are moving into the suburbs of Blauvain now, to begin their search.'

Ian reached out and pushed the annunciator stud again, holding it down as he spoke to the men inside.

'Are you coming out?'

'Why should we?' answered the voice that had spoken the first time. 'Give us a reason.'

'I'll come in and talk to you if you like,' said Ian.

'No –' began Pel out loud. I gripped his arm, and he turned on me, whispering. 'Tom, tell him not to go in! That's what they want.'

'Stay here,' I said.

I pushed forward until Charley ap Morgan put out an arm to stop me. I spoke across that arm to Ian.

163

'Ian,' I said, in a voice safely low enough so that the door annunciator would not pick it up. 'Pel says –'

'Maybe that's a good idea,' said the voice from the annunciator. 'That's right, why don't you come on in, Graeme? Leave your weapons outside.'

'Tom,' said Ian, without looking either at me or Charley ap Morgan, 'Stay back. Keep him back, Charley.'

'Yes sir,' said Charley. He looked into my face, eye to eye with me. 'Stay out of this, Tom. Back up.'

Ian stepped forward to stand square in front of the door, where a beam coming through it could go through him as well. He was taking off his sidearm as he went. He dropped it to the floor, in full sight of the screen, through the blankness of which those inside would be looking out.

'I'm unarmed,' he said.

'Of that sidepiece, you are,' said the annunciator. 'Do you think we're going to take your word for the rest of you? Strip.'

Without hesitation, Ian unsealed his uniform jacket and began to take off his clothes. In a moment or two, he stood naked in the hallway; but if the men in the suite had thought to gain some sort of moral advantage over him because of that, they were disappointed.

Stripped, he looked – like an athlete – larger and more impressive than he had, clothed. He towered over us all in the hall, even over the other Dorsai there; and with his darkly tanned skin under the lights he seemed like a massive figure carved in oak.

'I'm waiting,' he said, after a moment, calmly.

'All right,' said the voice from the annunciator. 'Come on in. '

He moved forward. The door unlatched and slid aside before him. He passed through and it closed behind him. For a moment we were left with no sound or word from him or the suite; then, unexpectedly, the screen lit up. We found ourselves looking over and past Ian's bare shoulders at a room in which three men, each armed with a rifle and a pair of sidearms, sat facing him. They gave no sign of knowing that he had turned on the annunciator screen, the controls of which would be hidden behind him, now that he stood inside the door, facing the room.

The center one of the three seated men laughed. He was the big, black-bearded man I had found vaguely familiar when I saw the solidigraphs of the three of them in Ian's office; and I recognized him now. He was a professional wrestler. He had been arraigned on assault charges four years ago, but lack of testimony against him had caused the charges to be dismissed. He was not as tall as Ian, but much heavier of body; and it was his voice we had been hearing, because now we heard it again as his lips moved on the screen.

'Well, well, Commander,' he said. 'Just what we needed – a visit from you. Now we can rack up a score of two Dorsai Commanders before your soldiers carry what's left of us off to the morgue; and St. Marie can see that even you people can be handled by the Blue Front.'

We could not see Ian's face; but he said nothing and apparently his lack of reaction was irritating to the big assassin, because he dropped his cheerful tone and leaned forward in his chair.

'Don't you understand, Graeme?' he said. 'We've lived and died for the Blue Front, all three of us – for the one political party with the strength and guts to save our world. We're dead men no matter what we do. Did you think we don't know that? You think we don't know what would happen to us if we were idiots enough to surrender the way you said? Your men would tear us apart; and if there was anything left of us after that, the government's law would try us and then shoot us. We only let you in here so that we could lay you out like your twin brother, before we were laid out ourselves. Don't you follow me, man? You walked into our hands here like a fly into a trap, never realizing.'

'I realized,' said Ian.

165

The big man scowled at him and the muzzle of the heat rifle he held in one thick hand, came up.

'What do you mean?' he demanded. 'Whatever you think you've got up your sleeve isn't going to save you. Why would you come in here, knowing what we'd do?'

'The Dorsai are professional soldiers,' said Ian's voice, calmly. 'We live and survive by our reputation. Without that reputation none of us could earn our living. And the reputation of the Dorsai in general is the sum of the reputations of its individual men and women. So Field Commander Kensie Graeme's professional reputation is a thing of value, to be guarded even after his death. I came in for that reason.'

The big man's eyes narrowed. He was doing all the talking and his two companions seemed content to leave it that way.

'A reputation's worth dying for?' he said.

'I've been ready to die for mine for eighteen years,' said Ian's voice, quietly. 'Today's no different than yesterday.'

'And you came in here –' the big man's voice broke off on a snort. 'I don't believe it. Watch him, you two!'

'Believe or not,' said Ian. 'I came in here, just as I told you, to see that the professional reputation of Field Commander Graeme was protected from events which might tarnish it. You'll notice –' his head moved slightly as if indicating something behind him and out of our sight, 'I've turned on your annunciator screen, so that outside the door they can see what's going on in here.'

The eyes of the three men jerked upwards to stare at the screen inside the suite, somewhere over Ian's head. There was a blur of motion that was Ian's tanned body flying through the air, a sound of something smashing and the screen went blank again.

We outside were left blind once more, standing in the hallway, staring at the unresponsive screen and door. Pel, who had stepped up next to me, moved toward the door itself.

'Stay!' snapped Charley.

The single sharp tone was like a command given to some domestic beast. Pel flinched at the tone, but stopped – and in that moment the door before us disintegrated to the roar of an explosion in the room.

'Come on!' I yelled, and flung myself through the now-open doorway.

It was like diving into a centrifuge filled with whirling bodies. I ducked to avoid the flying form of one of the men I had seen in the screen, but his leg slammed my head, and I went reeling, half-dazed and disoriented, into the very heart of the tumult. It was all a blur of action. I had a scrambled impression of explosions, of fire-beams lancing around me – and somehow in the midst of it all, the towering, brown body of Ian moving with the certainty and deadliness of a panther. All those he touched went down; and all who went down, stayed down.

Then it was over. I steadied myself with one hand against a half-burned wall and realized that only Ian and myself were on our feet in that room. Not one of the other Dorsai had followed me in. On the floor, the three assassins lay still. One had his neck broken. Across the room a second man lay obviously dead, but with no obvious sign of the damage that had ended his life. The big man, the ex-wrestler, had the right side of his forehead crushed in, as if by a club.

Looking up from the three bodies, I saw I was now alone in the room. I turned back into the corridor, and found there only Pel and Charley. Ian and the other Dorsai were already gone.

'Where's Ian?' I asked Charley. My voice came out thickly, like the voice of a slightly drunken man.

'Leave him alone,' said Charley. 'You don't need him, now. Those are the assassins there; and the enlisted men have already been notified and pulled back from their search of Blauvain. What more is needed?'

I pulled myself together; and remembered I was a policeman.

'I've got to know exactly what happened,' I said. 'I've

167

got to know if it was self-defense, or . . .'

The words died on my tongue. To accuse a naked man of anything else in the death of three heavily armed individuals who had threatened his life, as I had just heard them do over the annunciator, was ridiculous.

'No,' said Charley. 'This was done during a period of martial law in Blauvain. Your office will receive a report from our command about it; but actually it's not even something within your authority.'

Some of the tension that had been in him earlier seemed to leak out of him, then. He half-smiled and became more like the friendly officer I had known before Kensie's death.

'But that martial law is about to be withdrawn,' he said. 'Maybe you'll want to get on the phone and start getting your own people out here to tidy up the details.'

– And he stood aside to let me go.

One day later, and the professional soldiers of the Exotic Expeditionary Force showed their affection for Kensie in a different fashion.

His body had been laid in state for a public review in the open, main floor lobby of the Blauvain City Government building. Beginning in the grey dawn and through the cloudless day – the sort of hard, bright day that seems impatient with those who will not bury their dead and get on to further things – the mercenaries filed past the casket holding Kensie, visible at full length in dress uniform under the transparent cover. Each one as he passed touched the casket lightly with his fingertips, or said a word to the dead man, or both. There were over ten thousand soldiers passing, one at a time. They were unarmed, in field uniforms and their line seemed endless.

But that was not the end of it. The civilians of Blauvain had formed along either side of the street down which the line of troops wound on its way to the place where Kensie lay waiting for them. The civilians had formed in the face of strict police orders against doing any such thing; and my men could not drive them away. The situation could not have offered a better opportunity for the Blue Front to cause trouble. One heat grenade tossed into that line of slowly moving, unarmed soldiers, for example . . . But nothing happened.

By the time noon came and went without incident, I was ready to make a guess why not. It was because there was something in the mood of the civilian crowd itself that forbade terrorism, here and now. Any Blue Front activists trying such a thing would have been smothered by the very civilians around them in whose name they were doing it.

Something of awe and pity, and almost of envy, seemed to be stirring the souls of the Blauvain people; those same people of mine who had huddled in their houses twenty hours before, in undiluted fear of the very men now lined up before them and moving slowly to the City Government building. Once more, as I stood on a balcony above the lobby holding the casket, I felt those winds of vast movement I had sensed first for a moment in Ian's office, the winds of those forces of which Padma had spoken to me. The Blauvain people were different today and showed the difference. Kensie's death had changed them.

Then, something more happened. As the last of the soldiers passed, Blauvain civilians began to fall in behind them, extending the line. By mid-afternoon, the last soldier had gone by and the first figure in civilian clothes passed the casket, neither touching it nor speaking to it, but pausing to look with an unusual, almost shy curiosity upon the face of the body inside, in the name of which so much might have happened.

Already, behind that one man, the line of civilians was half again as long as the line of soldiers had been.

It was nearly midnight, long past the time when it had been planned to shut the gates of the lobby, when the last of the civilians had gone and the casket could be transferred to a room at Expeditionary Headquarters from which it would be shipped back to the Dorsai. This business of

169

shipping a body home happened seldom, even in the case of mercenaries of the highest rank; but there had never been any doubt that it would happen in the case of Kensie. The enlisted men and officers of his command had contributed the extra funds necessary for the shipment. – Ian, when his time came, would undoubtedly be buried in the earth of whatever world on which he fell. Only if he happened to be at home when the time came, would that earth be soil of the Dorsai. But Kensie had been – Kensie.

'Do you know what's been suggested to me?' asked Moro, as he, Pel and I, along with several of the Expedition's senior officers – Charley ap Morgan among them – stood watching Kensie's casket being brought into the room at Expedition HQ. 'There's a proposal to get the city government to put up a statue of him, here in Blauvain. A statue of Kensie.'

Neither Pel nor I answered. We stood watching the placing of the casket. For all its massive appearance, four men handled it and the body within easily. The apparently thick metal of its sides were actually hollow to reduce shipping weight. The soldiers settled it, took off the transparent weather cover and carried it out. The body of Kensie lay alone, uncovered; the profile of his face, seen from where we stood, quiet and still against the light pink cloth of the casket's lining. The senior officers who were with us and who had not been in the line of soldiers filing through the lobby, now began to go into the room, one at a time to stand for a second at the casket before coming out again.

'It's what we never had on St. Marie,' said Pel, after a long moment. He was a different man since Padma had talked to him. 'A leader. Someone to love and follow. Now that our people have seen there is such a thing, they want something like it for themselves.'

He looked up at Charley ap Morgan, who was just coming back out of the room.

'You Dorsai changed us,' Pel said.

'Did we?' said Charley, stopping. 'How do you feel about Ian now, Pel?'

'Ian?' Pel frowned. 'We're talking about Kensie. Ian's just – what he always was.'

'What you all never understood,' said Charley, looking from one to the other of us.

'Ian's a good man,' said Pel. 'I don't argue with that. But there'll never be another Kensie.'

'There'll never be another Ian,' said Charley. 'He and Kensie made up one person. That's what none of you ever understood. Now half of Ian is gone, into the grave.'

Pel shook his head slowly.

'I'm sorry,' he said. 'I can't believe that. I can't believe Ian ever needed anyone – even Kensie. He's never risked anything, so how could he lose anything? After Kensie's death he did nothing but sit on his spine here insisting that he couldn't risk Kensie's reputation by doing anything – until events forced his hand. That's not the action of a man who's lost the better half of himself.'

'I didn't say better half,' said Charley, 'I only said half – and just half is enough. Stop and try to feel for a moment what it would be like. Stop for a second and feel how it would be if you were amputated down the middle – if the life that was closest to you was wrenched away, shot down in the street by a handful of self-deluded, crackpot revolutionaries from a world you'd come to rescue. Suppose it was like that for you, how would you feel?'

Pel had gone a little pale as Charley talked. When he answered his voice had a slight echo of the difference and youngness it had had after Padma had talked to him.

'I guess . . .' he said very slowly, and ran off into silence.

'Yes?' said Charley. 'Now you're beginning to understand, to feel as Ian feels. Suppose you feel like this and just outside the city where the assassins of your brother are hiding there are six battalions of seasoned soldiers who can turn that same city – who can hardly be held

171

back from turning that city – into another Rochmont, at one word from you. Tell me, is it easy, or is it hard, not to say that one word that will turn them loose?'

'It would be . . .' The words seemed dragged from Pel, 'hard . . .'

'Yes,' said Charley, grimly, 'as it was hard for Ian.'

'Then why did he do it?' demanded Pel.

'He told you why,' said Charley. 'He did it to protect his brother's military reputation, so that not even after his death should Kensie Graeme's name be an excuse for anything but the highest and best of military conduct.'

'But Kensie was dead. He couldn't hurt his own reputation!'

'His troops could,' said Charley. 'His troops wanted someone to pay for Kensie's death. They wanted to leave a monument to Kensie and their grief for him, as long-lasting a monument as Rochmont has been to Jacques Chrétien. There was only one way to satisfy them, and that was if Ian himself acted for them – as their agent – in dealing with the assassins. Because nobody could deny that Kensie's brother had the greatest right of all to represent all those who had lost with Kensie's death.'

'You're talking about the fact that Ian killed the men, personally,' said Moro. 'But there was no way he could know he'd come face to face –'

He stopped, halted by the thin, faint smile on Charley's face.

'Ian was our Battle Op, our strategist,' said Charley. 'Just as Kensie was Field Commander, our tactician. Do you think that a strategist of Ian's ability couldn't lay a plan that would bring him face to face, alone, with the assassins once they were located?'

'What if they hadn't been located?' I asked. 'What if I hadn't found out about Pel, and Pel hadn't told us what he knew?'

Charley shook his head.

'I don't know,' he said. 'Somehow Ian must have

172

known this way would work – or he would have done it differently. For some reason he counted on help from you, Tom.'

'Me!' I said. 'What makes you say that?'

'He told me so.' Charley looked at me strangely. 'You know, many people thought that because they didn't understand Ian, that Ian didn't understand them. Actually, he understands other people unusually well. I think he saw something in you, Tom, he could rely on. And he was right, wasn't he?'

Once more, the winds I had felt – of the forces of which Padma had spoken, blew through me, chilling and enlightening me. Ian had felt those winds as well as I had – and understood them better. I could see the inevitability of it now. There had been only one pull on the many threads entangled in the fabric of events here; and that pull had been through me to Ian.

'When he went to that suite where the assassins were holed up,' said Charley, 'he intended to go in to them alone, and unarmed. And when he killed them with his bare hands, he did what every man in the Expeditionary force wanted to do. So, when that was done, the anger of the troops was lightning-rodded. Through Ian, they all had their revenge; and then they were free. Free just to mourn for Kensie as they're doing today. So Blauvain escaped; and the Dorsai reputation has escaped stain, and the state of affairs between the inhabited worlds hasn't been upset by an incident here on St. Marie that could make enemies out of worlds, like the Exotic and the Dorsai, and St. Marie, who should all be friends.'

He stopped talking. It had been a long speech for Charley; and none of us could think of anything to say. The last of the senior officers, all except Ian, had gone past us now, in and out of the room, and the casket was alone. Then Pel spoke.

'I'm sorry,' he said, and he sounded sorry. 'But even if what you say is all true, it only proves what I always said about Ian. Kensie had two men's feelings, but Ian hasn't any. He's ice and water with no blood in him. He couldn't bleed if he wanted to. Don't tell me any man torn apart emotionally by his twin brother's death could sit down and plan to handle a situation so cold-bloodedly and efficiently.'

'People don't always bleed on the outside where you can see –' Charley broke off, turning his head.

We looked where he was looking, down the corridor behind us, and saw Ian coming, tall and alone. He strode up to us, nodded briefly at us, and went past into the room. We saw him walk to the side of the casket.

He did not speak to Kensie, or touch the casket gently as the soldiers passing through the lobby had done. Instead he closed his big hands, those hands that had killed three armed men, almost casually on the edge of it, and looked down into the face of his dead brother.

Twin face gazed at twin face, the living and the dead. Under the lights of the room, with the motionless towering figure of Ian, it was as if both were living, or both were dead – so little difference there was to be seen between them. Only, Kensie's eyes were closed and Ian's opened; Kensie slept while Ian waked. And the oneness of the two of them was so solid and evident a thing, there in that room, that it stopped the breath in my chest.

For perhaps a minute or two Ian stood without moving. His face did not change. Then he lifted his gaze, let go of the casket and turned about. He came walking toward us, out of the room, his hands at his sides, the fingers curled into his palms.

'Gentlemen,' he said, nodding to us as he passed, and went down the corridor until a turn in it took him out of sight.

Charley left us and went softly back into the room. He stood a moment there, then turned and called to us.

'Pel,' he said, 'come here.'

Pel came; and the rest of us after him.

'I told you,' Charley said to Pel, 'some people don't bleed on the outside where you can see it.'

He moved away from the casket and we looked at it. On its edge were the two areas where Ian had laid hold of it with his hands while he stood looking down at his dead brother. There was no mistaking the places, for at both of them, the hollow metal side had been bent in on itself and crushed with the strength of a grip that was hard to imagine. Below the crushed areas, the cloth lining of the casket was also crumpled and rent; and where each fingertip had pressed, the fabric was torn and marked with a dark stain of blood.

Epilogue

'. . . So,' said the third Amanda, at last, 'you see how it really was.'

Hal Mayne nodded. He lifted his head suddenly to see her staring penetratingly at him.

'Or,' she said, 'do you see something more than I see, even in this?'

He opened his mouth to deny that, and found he could not.

'Maybe,' he said. Loneliness and a need to explain himself swept through him without warning, like a heavy tide. 'You've got to understand I'm a poet. I . . . I handle things all the time I don't understand. I'm almost like someone in total darkness, feeling things, sensing things, but never seeing shapes I can describe to other people.'

She breathed slowly, in and out.

'So,' she said, 'there was something more to this interest of yours in the ap Morgans and the Graemes, all along.'

'Yes . . . no!' he said, almost explosively. 'You still don't understand. I can't prove anything, but I can feel . . . connections.'

His hands moved, reached out almost as if by their own wills, to grasp at the empty air in front of him.

'Connections,' he said, 'between the past and the present. Between Cletus and Donal and many others, not related at all. Connections between you and the other two Amandas, and between the ap Morgans and the Graemes – and between all these things and the movement of the Splinter Culture cross-breeds – the New Kind, as they're calling themselves now – and the rest of

179

the human race on all the worlds. I'm fumbling in the dark, but I'm getting there . . . I can feel myself getting there!'

She had relaxed. She still watched him, but no longer accusingly.

'So that's why you have to head back now, to Earth and the Final Encyclopedia,' she said.

'Yes.' He looked at her starkly. 'I had to leave to save my life. But now, I have to go back. Everything on Coby, on Harmony, even everything here, keeps pointing me back there.'

He reached for her hand. She let him take it, but without returning the pressure of his fingers.

'Amanda,' he said urgently. 'Come back with me. I don't mean just because I want you with me. I mean because that's where all things are finally coming together. That's where it all ends – or starts. You should be there – just as I have to be there. Amanda, come with me.'

She sat still for a moment, then her eyes went past him. Gently, she withdrew her hand from his.

'If you're right, then I will come,' she said. 'But not now, Hal. Not now. In my own good time.'

The triumphant culmination of the Dorsai saga

THE FINAL ENCYCLOPAEDIA
Gordon R. Dickson

Winner of the Hugo and Nebula Awards

Almost a century has passed since the legendary Donal Graeme, master of interplanetary warfare and unifier of mankind, disappeared into the vastness of space. Out of his great vision only scattered colonies of the Dorsai, Earth, the Exotics and the Friendlies now remain to challenge the all-conquering Others who have mutated from the strongest of the Splinter Cultures to rule the galaxy.

Yet even these last bastions are in disarray, their peoples isolated and divided by self-interest. Only someone who can understand the forces of their long and glorious history – someone in whom the spirit of the Dorsai lives on – can bring them together against the new supermen and prove that their own evolution has not been in vain.

'A great hero in a great story.' *Frank Herbert*

SCIENCE FICTION   0 7221 3022 8   £3.99

DONALD MOFFITT

THE Genesis QUEST

A mighty, multi-dimensional, intergalactic epic

In a distant star system in the far future, the alien Nar species intercept messages from Earth revealing the secrets of human knowledge and culture. The sciences the Nar learn lead to technological breakthrough after breakthrough, until finally they can re-create human beings themselves.

A large human community evolves alongside the Nar, is encouraged to develop, grow and understand the mysteries of their galaxy. Only knowledge of Earth itself, millions of light years away, is prohibited. But one man, Bram, a bioengineer, dreams of travelling to Earth, and he is determined to achieve the impossible . . .

'Enthralling, mind-boggling, magnificent!' *Locus*

And don't miss the thrilling sequel:
SECOND GENESIS
also available in Sphere Books

0 7474 0015 6   SCIENCE FICTION   £3.50

A selection of bestsellers from SPHERE

FICTION

JUBILEE: THE POPPY CHRONICLES 1	Claire Rayner	£3.50 ☐
DAUGHTERS	Suzanne Goodwin	£3.50 ☐
REDCOAT	Bernard Cornwell	£3.50 ☐
WHEN DREAMS COME TRUE	Emma Blair	£3.50 ☐
THE LEGACY OF HEOROT	Niven/Pournelle/Barnes	£3.50 ☐

FILM AND TV TIE-IN

BUSTER	Colin Shindler	£2.99 ☐
COMING TOGETHER	Alexandra Hine	£2.99 ☐
RUN FOR YOUR LIFE	Stuart Collins	£2.99 ☐
BLACK FOREST CLINIC	Peter Heim	£2.99 ☐
INTIMATE CONTACT	Jacqueline Osborne	£2.50 ☐

NON-FICTION

BARE-FACED MESSIAH	Russell Miller	£3.99 ☐
THE COCHIN CONNECTION	Alison and Brian Milgate	£3.50 ☐
HOWARD & MASCHLER ON FOOD	Elizabeth Jane Howard and Fay Maschler	£3.99 ☐
FISH	Robyn Wilson	£2.50 ☐
THE SACRED VIRGIN AND THE HOLY WHORE	Anthony Harris	£3.50 ☐

All Sphere books are available at your local bookshop or newsagent, or can be ordered direct from the publisher. Just tick the titles you want and fill in the form below.

Name _____

Address _____

_____

Write to Sphere Books, Cash Sales Department, P.O. Box 11, Falmouth, Cornwall TR10 9EN

Please enclose a cheque or postal order to the value of the cover price plus:

UK: 60p for the first book, 25p for the second book and 15p for each additional book ordered to a maximum charge of £1.90.

OVERSEAS & EIRE: £1.25 for the first book, 75p for the second book and 28p for each subsequent title ordered.

BFPO: 60p for the first book, 25p for the second book plus 15p per copy for the next 7 books, thereafter 9p per book.

Sphere Books reserve the right to show new retail prices on covers which may differ from those previously advertised in the text elsewhere, and to increase postal rates in accordance with the P.O.